The Serpent's Call

Mason Marks

Chapter One

I.

Amazon Distribution Center—Atlanta, Georgia

November 1, 2024

1:00 p.m.

It's another day of packages. They flow through the warehouse in droves. I punch a clock here, the same as everyone else. The dullards surrounding me perform their duties with impeccable efficiency. They'll never tire of this monotony; you can see it in their eyes.

I'm standing next to a large bin of package envelopes, sorting through them one by one. I place them onto a tall, yellow tower with slots, ensuring that each continues toward its intended destination. It's all painfully mundane, but I can't say that I always hate it.

My escape calls to me. I fantasize about it often. My thoughts are filled with gasping pleas from unknown victims. Their muzzled suffering echoes within my mind as I cut pieces from their flesh.

"Asher. Hey, Asher!" Frank shouts. His voice is high and nasally; it grates my inner being. I've tried to ignore his attempts to gain my attention, but I'm no longer able. I draw myself from the fantasy and glare at him. Then

1

I push my long, dark hair back and await his explanation. He offers none. The man simply beckons me to follow him with an irritated hand gesture.

Scornfully, I comply. Frank straightens his tie and smirks behind a red complexion, watching me with dark, beady eyes. His mustache twitches while he wrinkles his nose.

Once he sees me following behind him, Frank tucks a clipboard by his side and then starts walking. As I walk behind him, my hatred begins to swell. Everything about him irks me deeply. His squeaking dress shoes, his short sleeve button-up, his stretched, blue slacks—they torment me from all angles while the venom grows inside.

We're approaching an office. I sigh quietly as I take in the familiar scenery: tall white walls, conveyor belts, bright yellow plastic containers, plastic subdividers that fence off portions of the distribution center, yellow guard rails, and hideous brown boxes as far as the eye can see.

We walk for a moment longer until we reach his office. It's completely nondescript. Everything, it seems, is either gray, black, or white. I stop at the doorway and check my phone. He's already sat down at his desk. The middle-aged man clears his throat to gain my attention. I glance at him tiredly through the large window and then proceed through the doorway.

"Have a seat," Frank orders as he gestures with his fat, hairy arm.

I sit. His chair is brown, leathery, and luxurious. Mine is plastic and metal. I look down at my navy blue uniform, lick my finger, and wipe off a small stain on my chest. I notice my hands. They seem paler than usual; they're discolored by the warm blood flowing through them. I haven't eaten in days and even my fingers are growing thin. I examine the dirt beneath my long cuticles.

"This is the third time this month," he warns. Frank lays a spreadsheet on his desk and then places a finger on it. "I've told you before. Our system traces every single error back to its point of origin. You, Mr. Asher, are that point of origin. Again. And it's been far too many times already," he chides me. "What's it going to take? How can I get through to you?" he asks, staring at me with baleful eyes. His awful mustache twitches while he awaits my response.

"I'm trying, Frank. I'm doing my best."

"Well, we're going to have to do better than that," he replies, easing up in his demeanor. "This is Amazon. People trust us, and we can't keep that trust if we're always sending packages to the wrong address." He raises his eyebrows to emphasize his point.

"I understand."

"Good. Then understand this: we can't keep you on if you continue making mistakes. There are people lined up around the block to work here."

"Yes, I can see that. You're right."

Frank sighs and then shakes his head. "Okay, carry on, then," he says at last, motioning with his hand as he looks away from me.

After a few seconds, we each stand up and head toward the door. I begin walking down the hallway alone. I'm heading back to my work station when I hear him grumbling behind me. Frank stands near the end of the hall with his hands on his hips, watching me as I go.

II.

Mickey's Pub and Grill

November 1, 2024

11:00 p.m.

I'm free now, and the hunt has only begun. It hasn't yet reached any point of exhilaration. I'm merely basking in the calm, early stages of it. The feeling of the chase warms my body as I breathe deeply and purge the day's stress from my lungs.

These grounds are fertile. They teem with game. Men, women, young, old—their type alone doesn't matter. None of these distinctions mean anything to me. All I want is their sorrow, profound and endless. I gaze around the room and imagine them all tied—bound for my pleasure. I think of their screams. They beg for mercy while I stand over them with sharpened metal.

There is one variable that matters above all. They must be vulnerable. Little loose threads, ready for me to pull on. They don't *have* to be alone, but it certainly helps. If they're not alone, though, there must be a way to separate them, to make them all mine.

I turn the base of a small sipping glass against the wood of the bar. I study the whiskey inside as it swirls against the glass. It's my nourishment for the evening. The liquor tastes like shit, and the rest of the bar is a cesspool, but it all brings me satisfaction, nonetheless.

The air around me buzzes with a faint hum. Television. Sports. The announcers' voices come in solidarity as a mass of white noise. Two older men are seated next to me. They are enthralled with the game, chatting with one another while eating peanuts from the bar. I seem to have hit a lull in my pace for the evening, so I stand up and head to the restroom.

I'm lost in my thoughts as I make my way through the bar. Once inside in the bathroom, I relieve myself inside a dingy, brown toilet. It looks as though it hasn't been scrubbed in years. Graffiti and faded markings cover the stall door and walls. After I finish, I walk out and stop in front of the bathroom mirror; it's broken with a large crack down the center that spreads across the glass.

I study my appearance without emotion. I'm wearing a red and black flannel shirt, dark blue jeans, and a pair of black leather boots. My eyes are empty and gray. A smirk spreads slowly across my face when I think of the payoff to come. I must steel my nerves. This portion of my task will make it all worthwhile in the end.

I head back toward the bar at a leisurely pace. I take my time and study everyone inside as I walk past them. Two couples sit at a table on a double date; they certainly won't do. Handfuls of girls and guys lean against the bar or stand in the large open area, but they're all paired up in some way. The timing simply isn't right yet. I turn the corner and head back toward my seat.

The two older men are still eating peanuts and watching television. But there is someone new. A man. He's a sick, little rat. He's hunched over and squinting to see his phone. He sits a few stools down from me. His head bobs with a gentle swing. Something about his morose attitude draws me in. I watch him for a moment; he glares angrily at his cellphone and seems to be expending all mental energy as he struggles to type.

"Hard times, brother?" I ask him in a cool, friendly tone.

He looks at me, surprised by the question. I'd put him at maybe forty-five. He is out of shape, but not fat—just a loose set of skin hanging from bones. His hairline is receding far onto his head; his hair is an unpredictable, greasy patchwork. He can't be taller than 5'6. "Nah, man, it's just this bitch..." he replies, taking his time.

"Women can be difficult," I sympathize.

"You said it," he slurs in a sloppy southern drawl. "She cheated on me right in front of me, dude. Just made out with some guy."

"Is she still here?" I ask, glancing around the bar.

He looks at me skeptically at first, but I suppose the booze has loosened him up. "No. Took an Uber home, I guess." He takes a long swig from his beer and then continues typing into his phone.

"Well, shit...let me buy you a round, then," I offer.

I order two bottom shelf whiskeys. The bartender pours them and brings the glasses over. I grab each of them and then migrate to the stool next to him.

The man looks up from his phone and purses his lips. "Can't say I'm about to turn that down," he says, tilting his head. "Name's Taylor. Taylor Hawkins."

"Good to meet you, Taylor. I'm Dalton," I reply, nodding as I offer him the glass.

Taylor takes the glass from my hand and smiles. "Cheers," he says, raising his drink.

We sit together for some time. Gradually, he begins opening up more and more as I buy drinks for the two of us. He doesn't seem to question my motives—it's odd how rarely they do. "So, what do you do?" I ask him.

"Construction," Taylor says. He stares into the TV for a moment before adding, "Just building nice houses for all the rich assholes."

"Must be nice," I reply, smirking.

"Yeah, nice for *them*," he goes on. "But yep, I do it all. Painting, woodwork, whatever needs to be done. Jack of all trades, really. What about you? What kind of work you do?"

"The boring kind," I reply, looking down at my drink. "I sort mail. It's not always bad, but my boss can be a real prick."

Taylor grunts and then takes a long swig from a bottle of beer. "He can't be worse than mine, just can't be..." he says with a drunken smile, shaking his head. "Cheap bastard's always cutting my hours."

We continue talking for another fifteen minutes or so. He's visibly inebriated. I've earned his trust and lowered his defenses, both of which are critical to the task at hand. He and I are alike in many ways, but that doesn't prevent my disdain. It will not impede my errand.

Even if Taylor were my friend, what would he and I do together? I can't imagine it. I find it difficult to listen to the man's ramblings as I imagine cutting his head off with a butcher's knife. I'd pull his hair and work my forearm with vigor, then pull it clean off the slate, and raise it ceremoniously in front of me. I can't help but dwell on the thought for what seems like several minutes. Eventually, I pull myself back to reality. He's telling me a longwinded story that sounds as though it's midway through.

Eye contact, that's the key. No one ever guesses what you're thinking when you're able to maintain it. It's a skill worth learning. They rarely suspect any ill intentions when they think they have this portal into your soul. But my soul belongs to another, and this cretinous being could never lift the veil—no matter how hard he tried.

Taylor delivers the punchline to his story and then begins laughing to himself as he awaits my response. I conjure up a meager string of laughter, but he seems disappointed by it. My placid veneer is starting to wear quite thin. We sit for nearly a minute in silence. He begins looking around the room for something to observe, something to say. When he can't manage to find it, he checks the time on his cell phone.

"Well, shit, partner, I didn't realize it'd gotten to be this late," he says. I can see on his phone that it's 2:05 a.m. "It's been nice to meet you, though, Halton."

"Likewise," I reply. I don't bother correcting him; instead, I smile and extend my hand to shake his.

He shakes my hand and nods with a friendly smile.

"Well, all right, let me get out of here...time to take my drunk ass to bed." He guffaws to himself before polishing off his last drink. "Thanks for the rounds!" he says. Taylor stands up slowly and starts patting his jacket pockets with a look of mild confusion on his face.

"Any time," I answer flatly.

He turns and begins heading toward the bar's exit. I watch him behind cold, gray eyes. My icy stare follows him all the way to the door. Once outside, he begins rummaging through his pockets. I can see him through the glass panes of the door. He pulls out an electronic cigarette and turns left on the sidewalk.

I take my time and begin heading toward the exit as well. Once I reach the door, I peek my head out; thankfully, he's still in my line of sight. He's bustling down the sidewalk with his right hand in his coat pocket. He's vaping with the left as his head hangs low.

My pursuit has begun. Taylor makes no effort to mind his surroundings. He exudes a lazy self-assurance. *Nothing will ever touch me,* he must be thinking. They're always my favorite. But something can, and something will reach out, dear friend—just far enough to clench you. And it happens tonight.

III.

Sidewalk Near Hillside Grove Apartments

November 2, 2024

2:15 a.m.

We've walked for about five minutes now. Taylor's just as careless as when we first set out. He's stumbling along and paying scarce attention. The man nearly bumps into fellow pedestrians as he continues dragging himself along with minimal effort or awareness.

Another five minutes pass. Taylor stops at a crosswalk across the street from a brown apartment complex. I stop a good twenty feet or so away from him. I try to look busy as we wait. The light changes, and he begins crossing the street. I start moving with him. Taylor pulls his phone from his pocket; he looks at it for a few seconds before dropping it onto the asphalt. "Ah, shit," he mutters to himself.

As Taylor bends down to retrieve his fallen phone, he spots me advancing toward him. *Goddammit,* I'm thinking—why couldn't you just keep your eyes forward? My expression betrays my surprise when his eyes fall upon me. He picks up the phone and waits for me to continue walking. "Halton...fancy seein' you here," he says with a stupid, drunken grin. Taylor places the phone back into his pocket; his body sways gently in the cold winter night.

"Yeah, small world," I mumble. *How could I be so feckless and sloppy?*

"Say...you're not following me, are ya?" The smile widens across his face.

"No," I reply, smiling as I feign a light chuckle, "I just live out this way too."

We stop near the curb after we reach the opposite side of the crosswalk. "Oh yeah, whereabouts?" he questions me good-naturedly.

I hardly know the area at all. My thoughts race as I try to come up with a plausible answer. I glance across the street. There's a brick entrance with a sign that reads, "Hillside Grove Apartments." I point to it and say, "Just down the street, actually."

"No way! So do I," Taylor replies. "Damn, what a coincidence. How'd that not come up before?"

"I'm not sure," I tell him. "That's really funny, though." I smile and nod. My calm, gentle expression raises no alarm inside the tired drunkard's skull. He's peaceful as a lamb.

Taylor and I continue toward the neighborhood entrance and then turn left. We walk through it and cross into a parking lot in front of the first set of apartments. Two rows of late model cars line the lot.

"This is me, right here," Taylor tells me, gesturing toward his apartment. He glances between the other buildings. "Where's yours?"

"Ah, mine's farther back. It's toward the end," I say, pointing down a winding street.

"Cool," he replies, gazing into the distance. "Well, hey, maybe we should get together again sometime."

"Yeah, that sounds good. Anyway, I'll see you later!" I tell him as I wave goodbye. Then I start heading in the direction I'd pointed to before.

Taylor starts ambling toward the first complex on the left. I glance over my shoulder and watch him as I walk away. Then I scan the area for a place to hide and spot a couple of dumpsters up ahead. I walk quickly toward them.

There's a brick wall surrounding the dumpsters. I hide behind it and then peek my head around the corner, watching Taylor as he approaches the last door on the left. He's pretty far away from me, at least a hundred feet or so. But even from this distance, I can make out the numbers on his door. "111," it reads in large, silver numbers.

Taylor stops in front of his door and pulls a key ring from his pocket. The porch light shines upon his face as he picks out the appropriate key. *Hurry up,* I'm thinking. I don't want to be spotted by some meddling imbecile taking out their trash late at night. I want to be clean, undetected.

Should I go now? I wonder. *No.* No, it's best to wait. Give him time to settle in. Time to fall asleep. Time to find himself in the exact position that I want him in. I glance down at my phone and note the time.

With about an hour to kill, I start walking. I head out of the neighborhood and then find myself back on the sidewalk. There's a late-night diner up ahead. I smile as the bright neon lights call my name.

I feel more tired than drunk as I begin making my way down the street. Still, I need to sober up. I've got to be attentive and at my very best, so I stop in an alleyway just before the diner. I look around to make sure that no one is watching me. Then I force myself to vomit onto the brick wall between two buildings.

After several iterations of me forcing my fingers down my throat, I am satisfied; the purge is empowering. I stare at the gelatinous vomit trail as it drips down the wall. Something about it is significant to me. I hold my gaze for a moment longer, but I cannot admire it for long. There are many things yet to do before the night is up. It's time to focus.

I approach the diner. Inside, it's brightly lit, and a large neon sign with cursive writing hangs above the entrance. There are only a few scattered customers sitting around as I walk through the door. A black sign by the register reads, "Please seat yourself." I comply.

As I make my way toward a table in the back, two couples sitting together in a booth suddenly stop talking. They eyeball me suspiciously. I suppose I look ruffled, so I run my fingers through my hair as I take my seat.

As I look around, I notice that the diner is quaint and greasy. I pick up a menu from the little metal stand on the table. Its many pictures of hamburgers, omelets, and hashbrowns sicken me to no end. I think perhaps I made a mistake by coming in.

No. I need the time to think. Coffee, that'll be my answer. A little black energy will clear my head right up.

The waitress walks over, and I order a cup. She seems disappointed to hear that's all I'm having. She's wearing a black apron with the restaurant's name etched into the corner. Her dirty blonde hair hangs in a messy bun as she stares behind black rimmed glasses. She walks slowly toward the kitchen area and retrieves the coffee pot and a gray mug. She pours it in front of me. I smile to her, conveying my normalcy. *See? I'm just like you.*

Now that I have my coffee, I can meditate upon the evening's plans. Someone might remember Taylor and me sitting next to each other at the bar. They'd remember us talking. But does that matter? It could. It might. But I need this. I can't deny that. It's been far too long, and I feel invested by this point. It's hard to walk away from the table in situations like these.

It matters, it doesn't matter, *who cares?* The truth is, I've been in this gutter of a city for long enough. It's probably time to hit the road soon, anyway. I've been doing my business here for quite some time now. How long has it been? I wonder as I pour two sugars into my black coffee. I stir it as the answer comes to me: nine months. Nine awful months in Atlanta. It seems longer.

The job isn't going well, anyway. I may not last much longer there. It's not even just my supervisor. I can't seem to blend in there like I could before. So yes, a move may be in order. A move away from my fat, stubby manager. A move away from this endless traffic and false hope. Regardless, I cannot let tonight's opportunity pass. I already know where Taylor lives. And I know that he will be alone tonight.

We must move forward, I decide, looking into the distance. After all, my personal needs are not the only ones to be considered. The Dark Lord is depending on his servant's resolve, and I shall not shrink from my duty.

IV.

Downtown Atlanta

November 2, 2024

2:55 a.m.

I've departed the diner, and I'm back on the streets now, heading toward Taylor's apartment. I've already entered his neighborhood, and I'm approaching his building. I scan the parking lot as I walk with my head down. There's no sign of anyone, not at this hour. It's nearly 3:00 a.m., and not a soul stirs but mine.

I didn't bring my usual kit with me. There's no time to go back home and retrieve it, either. But I do have a small lock pick inside my coat pocket. I try to carry it with me at all times. It comes in handy more often than you could imagine. It's not much bigger than a wallet, and it normally grants me all the access I need.

I reach inside my coat pocket and pull it out. Then I tear open the Velcro and take out the necessary tools. At the front door, I fumble around for a few minutes, trying to ease my way inside. I'm nervous, I must admit. I'm not immune to it. My senses are raised. I hear, smell, and taste everything around me as I twist and prod the lock with my small metal rods. After a moment, I feel it suddenly click; relief washes over me as I turn the handle.

I walk inside. The interior of Taylor's apartment is predictably plain. It has beige carpets and walls. A small TV and a brown couch sit at the center of his living room. There's almost no decoration whatsoever. I wish I'd planned this out better, thought further ahead. I usually scout a location over several days and then come prepared with all the necessary tools. But tonight, I need it. And I need it quickly—not tomorrow, nor the day after. I'm *far* overdue. My desire has risen to an untenable level.

There's no motion inside the apartment. It's complete desolation of night. White noise fills my ears as I draw a black six-inch knife from my boot and walk through the living room. I head toward the hallway with caution. The door at the end is cracked open. I advance toward it, peek inside, and there he is, sleeping. The unwary oaf is passed out, snoring with his mouth open. It seems time is on my side, then.

I creep back through the hallway, careful not to make a sound in the dreadful silence. What to do, what to do? I think to myself. How should I...*ah-ha*! There it is. He's a handyman. A construction guy. He's bound to have a few things lying around here that will be useful. Indeed, he must.

I look around the living room, and its practically barren. But there's a small closet to the right of the couch. I walk toward it and open the door. *What have we here?* A small green duffel bag is half-zipped and sitting on the floor.

There's almost nothing else inside the closet, so I pull the bag out and begin rummaging through it. I find a hammer, a box cutter, several screw drivers, a small handsaw, and a power drill. I smile to myself and take stock of it all. There's a plastic kit with assorted nails and screws too, along with various types of wall patches. A few unused paintbrushes are scattered inside the bag as well. I check the rest of the closet too, but there's nothing of use; it's just clothes and several gallons of paint.

Hmm...we're still missing something. He's got to have it here some-where—I know he does. I head into the kitchen. It's as unimpressive as the rest of his abode. No matter. I slide open a few drawers next to the sink and find what I'm looking for: tape. A beautiful, thick roll of duct tape. I hold it in front of me and smile. The air tastes refreshing as I admire its silver promise. I place the roll into my coat pocket, then return my boot knife to its sheath.

I walk over to the kitchen table and stand behind one of the chairs. I shake it to test its sturdiness. "That'll do," I whisper. It even has arms! Despite my lack of preparation, everything seems as though it'll work just fine. And yet, something stops me from moving forward.

I walk back down the hallway and gently open the second bedroom door. It appears to be an office or perhaps a man-cave. There's a desk along the righthand wall with a computer and office chair. On the opposite side, there's a recliner and a television in the corner.

I can't help but notice all of his décor. The Atlanta Braves. Their memorabilia covers nearly the entire wall behind his desk. A framed set of baseball cards hangs proudly. A catcher's mitt is mounted beneath a baseball bat on the wall. Both have several signatures scrawled upon them. I take the bat from its place on the wall and test its weight, extending it all the way out, and then tossing it up with one hand. It's always good to have a blunt object.

I think we're ready. I have only the vaguest plan sketched out in my mind as I leave the room and approach his bedroom door once again. Still there, I see. Taylor's mouth hangs open. I doubt anyone could wake this man without considerable effort. I can tell that he's not dreaming—not a single thought passes through his empty mind as I examine him. Nonetheless, I proceed with caution once I come closer.

I glance around the room, and unsurprisingly, it's quite messy. Dirty clothes are strewn about the floor, and he's sleeping on a mattress on the ground. His window is missing a set of blinds, and there's a large crack that runs through it like a spider web.

Gently, I bend over and look into his sleeping face. He's lying on his stomach. The blanket only covers him halfway, and I can see that he's wearing a pair of gray sweatpants and white socks. I listen to him breathe. His chest rises and falls in a peaceful rhythm. His snoring is deep and regular.

Taylor's lips quiver while he sleeps; he's completely unaware of my presence...or of what's to come. I keep my eyes fixed on him as I reach into my coat pocket and pull out the roll of duct tape. I begin unspooling it slowly; I mustn't wake him with its loud tearing sound.

After I have a piece that's around eight inches long, I return the spool to my pocket and move closer to him. Then I tuck the bat under my elbow and stretch the piece out horizontally, ready to make my move. Tenderly, I place it upon his lips. His nose twitches and the rhythmic breathing stops. Don't do it, I think to myself; be at peace, little lamb.

But as I am settling into this notion of getting what I want, I see his sleepy eyes begin to open. *Fuck.* Why can't things ever be easy? His drowsy eyes quickly take focus on the shadowy figure standing above him; he looks up at me with alarm. Taylor tries shouting, not yet realizing that his mouth has been taped shut.

I raise the bat overhead and bring it crashing down upon his legs. I don't want him mobile. I need him to be mine—my compliant little offering. Taylor tries to scream, but his sounds are muffled beneath the tape. His agony has just begun.

I breathe deeply, taking in the foul stench of his apartment. It's always so rewarding once the suffering has commenced. But I cannot fully take my time, because Taylor is now shuffling in bed, trying to make his escape.

But I can't allow that; our fun hasn't even started. He's managed to get to his knees and is trying to crawl toward the door. His hands are scouring the floor, and he's knocking things over on the dresser while searching for some instrument of defense. I teach him his place by smacking his right hand hard with the bat. He howls in pain and then turns over on his back, clutching his hand.

As Taylor grips his injured hand, I walk toward him calmly. He's looking up at me in confusion, in fear. He tears the tape off with his good hand. I'm standing over him now, and he tries wriggling his hips around to create a little distance between us, but I won't let him. Every inch he moves, I move with him. The bat is lowered by my side in one hand. It's dark in his room, but the light coming in from the window illuminates my face just enough for him to recognize me. "Halton? What...what the fuck?!"

I shake my head, chiding him in silence. "No talking," I mutter.

"Get the fuck out of here!" he shouts before I strike him with the bat again. Taylor's rolling on the ground now, using his arms to try to stop my blows. He screams in between each one, and that only makes me hit him harder and faster. *Shut the fuck up, you coward.*

One by one, they come crashing down, and he's quickly losing all sense of self-preservation. I don't hit him in the head, because I don't want to risk killing him at this early stage. There's still so much more to do. Taylor's lying motionless on the ground. He won't look at me anymore. He's staring off to one side, sniveling, and holding a bruised, shaky hand up to his face.

I grab both of Taylor's feet and begin dragging him toward the doorway. He's dazed and looking aimlessly around the room as it passes him by. Taylor sticks a hand out when we cross through the threshold; he's trying to grab ahold of the doorframe. But by this point, his strength is all but gone, and his grip gives way immediately.

I drag his deflated body down the hallway. We make it into the kitchen, and I catch my breath for a moment as I rest my boot on top of his chest. He's looking around the room and getting ideas, I can tell. But before he can devise any clever plot to save his own miserable life, I start raising him up by the armpits. I hoist him up with considerable effort as he's all dead weight beneath me. I lift him up just enough to place him into the wooden chair in the dining room by the kitchen.

Once his back hits the chair, he immediately tries to sit up. He launches his arms out and leans forward. His desperate eyes focus on the doorway behind me to the right. I hold him down with one hand and use the other to thump him on the head with the bat. He reels back, placing a hand on his head. Then I pull the tape out and secure his other arm to the chair. Taylor sees me doing this and suddenly forgets about all the pain that he's in. He begins trying to hit me with his free hand.

I drop the bat and grab his arm with both hands. We struggle against each other briefly, but he's too weak to resist me now. I force his hand onto the arm of the chair and then pick up the roll of duct tape from the floor. I keep his arm pinned as I begin unspooling a long stretch of tape. Then I use it to secure his remaining arm. He starts screaming, "Help! Goddammit! Help! Let me go, faggot! What the fuck is wrong with you?!"

I smirk as I stand over him. "Oh, I promise, my interest in you isn't sexual." I take the roll of tape and apply a fresh piece to his mouth. Taylor begins moving around, using the movement of his hips to rock the chair back and forth. He's trying to jump out of his bondage, but I cannot allow that. I watch him squirm as I think about how to remedy the situation.

I walk over to the closet in the corner of his living room. Then I grab the duffel bag of tools that I found earlier and take it over to Taylor. He's still shuffling around, and it's time to show him the permanency of his situation.

I take the plastic kit of nails from the bag and then pull out the hammer. I open the kit and find the longest nails that I can. Then I take a few of them and walk over to Taylor, crouching by his feet with the hammer in hand. He begins trying to kick me, though he can't gain the momentum to do any real damage. He's defenseless, but still annoying.

Taylor doesn't wish to be subordinate, yet he must be. I strike his foot hard with the hammer. His head shoots up as he writhes in pain. I strike both of his feet several times for good measure. They've now fallen limp and offer me no more resistance. I take both of his feet in hand, placing one on top of the other.

Then I position a nail on top of Taylor's foot and drive it in deep with the hammer. It doesn't go all the way through to the floor, but his feet are fastened together. His legs begin kicking wildly, and I can see tears streaming down his face. I grab his adjoined feet and nail the bottom one to the carpet.

Taylor looks defeated. His head sags off to one side. Drool begins flowing under the silver tape. During our brief moment of calm, I take another nail and drive it into his hand. A small pool of blood forms on top as the metal pushes through the wood of the chair. It keeps him firmly in place. By this point, he's powerless, but I repeat the process anyway and nail his other hand down.

I take a step back and examine Taylor for a moment. Something about the scene's symmetry draws me in. Taylor won't look at me, but that is often the case—as if all of this were something *personal*, some vendetta against him specifically. But it's not. I'm simply performing my diligence. Must I do this? Yes, but that is beside the point. Something greater than the two of us is at work here.

I draw the knife from my boot once more. Then I place my hand on Taylor's shoulder and stab him in the ribs. I can feel the blade pressing against bone as I force it in as deep as it can go. Then I twist the knife to widen his wound. He's struggling against me, trying to move his shoulders as much as he can. But it's of no use, he's going nowhere.

I wipe the knife clean with his hair before placing it back inside my boot. Then I go to the tool bag and remove one of the paintbrushes. I place my hand on Taylor's head and force it against the top of the chair. Then I jam the paintbrush deep inside his wound.

I pull the brush out slowly, ensuring that I keep a coat of his thick, dark blood upon its bristles. It drips from the tip of the brush as I remove it. I swirl it gently to dry the edges while I walk to the wall behind Taylor. I paint a large circle on the blank wall; it takes most of the blood to do so. Then I walk back over to Taylor and jam the brush inside him again. He squirms and yells at me with his eyes while I gather another coat.

I return to the wall, painting a few hasty lines inside the circle. Then I stand back and admire it: an inverted pentagram scrawled in blood against a white canvas. I set the paintbrush down on the dining room table and kneel before the symbol with my head hanging low.

"Morning Star, with thy dreaded legions and unconquerable might, I beg you to bleed our greatest enemy. Rip the sanctimonious tyrant from his unearned throne. Drag him through the caverns of Hell, and chain him as he hath done to you. Father Satan, give us your black reign." I breathe deeply, and a warm, cleansing feeling pulses throughout my body. "*Ave Satanas,*" I whisper.

<h1 style="text-align:center">V.</h1>

Inside Taylor's Apartment
November 2, 2024
3:30 a.m.

I'm still kneeling beneath the pentagram when I open my eyes and look over at Taylor; he's glaring at me, confused. No matter, dear boy, you'll have your answers soon enough. I wish we could have made greater ceremony, you and I, but we must make do with what's available.

I draw my knife, stand back up, and then walk over to Taylor. I loom over him with the blade in hand. He looks up at me with pleading eyes; tears well in the corners of them while he shakes his head, begging for relief.

"I won't bother apologizing," I tell him. "The truth is, I need your pain, your suffering. It strengthens me, and it will strengthen *him*." I nod toward the wall with the freshly painted pentagram. "And at this point, that need far outweighs any point of pretense."

I take the knife and dig it into Taylor's forearm. I press it in deep and begin dragging it in a straight line. Then I make three turns with the blade while I carve a rough square upon his skin. Taylor's screaming through the tape, but I pay him no mind; I mustn't allow him to distract me from the task at hand. I take the edge of the blade and lift his flap of skin, carefully removing it from the arm. Once I have it, I set my bloody knife down on the table and examine his severed flesh.

I reach into the bag of tools and pull out the hammer and a single nail. I walk them over to the bloody pentagram, placing his skin in the center. Then I hammer it into the wall three times. And there it rests—my humble offering.

I hear the chair rocking back and forth as I look back at Taylor. He's still resisting. He still hasn't accepted the state of things. Even with his feet nailed to the floor and his hands attached to the chair, he fights.

I try not to let it bother me, but it does. I must show him. I must teach him his place. The hammer is still in my grasp, and I use it to bash the fingers on his left hand. Over and over, my instrument comes crashing down. It grows bloody while his fingers break beneath it; they protrude in horrifying, unnatural positions.

I can hear him weeping as soon as I stop my onslaught. His skin hangs loosely from the bone, and the chair is a bloody mess as it drips upon the carpet. "Do you see, my friend? Can you feel your fate?" He screams at me with what I can only assume are muted obscenities.

I reach inside the bag of tools and pull out the handsaw. How convenient, I think to myself. Taylor is protesting vehemently, shaking his head back and forth. I look into his eyes and grin as I place the serrated blade upon his right wrist. He screams as I begin moving the saw back and forth.

Taylor convulses in distress while I continue cutting into his arm, but after about thirty seconds of strained effort, I finish sawing my way through. His hand is severed, and I cut into the wood of the chair. His large, open wound bleeds just below the wrist.

Taylor's severed hand remains nailed to the chair, but his arm hangs freely now. He studies it with alarm. His panic surges while his eyes grow wider. The man can't choke out a single word; he just stares in disbelief as he curls the arm up to his face.

His blood flows consistently. It starts covering the carpet below. I can see the light starting to fade from his eyes. He grows weary once his adrenaline begins to wane; he starts settling into shock. The man's eyelids grow heavy, his jaw is slackened, and his head bobs aimlessly. Soon, the comfort of forced sleep takes him over. Taylor's head sags to the left, and finally, he's out.

Though my new friend has fallen asleep during our visit, I do not hold it against him. I kick Taylor's leg several times to wake him up, but he's out cold. I must say, it's disappointing that he'd choose to rest during such an important moment of his life, but that is his choice, not mine.

So be it. I will do what I can to preserve his life for the time being. I walk to Taylor's bedroom and take a belt from a pair of pants that I find lying on the floor. Then I wrap both ends of the belt around my hands and stretch the leather tight.

I head back toward the dining room with the leather in hand and fasten it around Taylor's arm. I pull and tug on the strap until I'm certain that it's restricted his blood flow. That should help. It'll keep him alive long enough for my purposes, anyway.

I look down at Taylor's nailed hand. Then I tug on it a few times before tearing it off the arm of the chair. The nail cuts into his dead flesh as I wrestle it free. I pick it up by one of the fingers. It feels like a child's plaything as it dangles in the air. I shake it up and down with some amusement as a large smile spreads across my face.

I take Taylor's severed hand to an end table that's beneath the pentagram, placing it ceremoniously in the center. I notice that he has two candles on a cart in the corner of the room. He's a man of culture after all. I bring them over to the end table and light them. It's all arranged in a beautiful display. I admire it proudly, nodding with contentment.

It is time for Taylor to rejoin the party, and I can think of only one way to ensure that happens. I head into his kitchen and search for what I am sure must be there. I reach into a cabinet above his refrigerator, and there it is: a half-drunk bottle of Jim Beam.

I sip from the bottle as I reapproach the sleeping man. I lean over and spit some of the liquor in his face, spewing it all out in good fun. There's no motion, it doesn't even register with him. Well, I figured that wouldn't do the trick by itself, but that wasn't really my intention. I dump the rest of the bottle onto his head and splash a little on his legs and torso.

I set the bottle down and retrieve a lighter from the end table. Then I lean down and spark it next to his face. The whiskey splashed all over him catches immediately. The flames travel up and down his body like the ripples of a wave. He's engulfed now, wide awake, and flailing his free arm in the air. He struggles to break free but finds himself unable—the nails and tape hold him firmly in place.

The flames have begun consuming Taylor's hair. His expression contorts as he squirms in the chair. The flesh on his face begins charring, and the tape that held his mouth closed has started melting into his lips. The fire burns holes into his sweatpants while it mars his chest. The man's frantic jaw movements finally tear the melted tape apart, and he's able to scream again.

The symphony of his anguish relieves me. I cannot help but enjoy it; I stand in majestic peace now, breathing deeply with my arms outstretched. But when his screams continue drawing themselves out, I bring myself back to the present moment. I cannot allow him to be so loud. This will get me caught.

I pick the bat off the floor and then swing it with one arm, striking hard him on the temple. Out he goes again. I take a moment to calm myself as silence fills the room. Taylor's head is sagging onto his chest. His face is bleeding and blackened in large, uneven spots. His hair is a messy, charred swirl. It's all so invigorating.

What now? More fire? *No.* That's far too redundant. And as much as I'd enjoy carving him to pieces and reveling in his slow demise, I must be cautious still. Perhaps it's time to get to the heart of the matter.

I pick up the knife from the table next to me. Then I lift Taylor's slumped head by the chin. His blackened wounds are still bleeding, and it makes a mess of my wrist and hands. I rear the knife back and then jam it forcefully into his eye socket. I start digging the blade in deeper as Taylor awakens, howling in hysterics.

I slice through the optic nerve and then pull his eye from the socket with my free hand. I set it on the table next to me. His head is jerking back and forth in violent spasms while I take hold of him again. I jam my knife into the other socket and repeat the process. His panic grows to a new height, and he's unable to scream any longer. All that comes from his lips are choked stammers; it's like an indecipherable creaking. As the eyeless man struggles to catch his breath, I can practically see his heart beating out of his chest.

Once more, I draw back with the knife, this time shoving it deep inside his mouth. His lips begin opening and closing as I dig around inside. I use my free hand to reach in and tear the tongue from his gushing orifice. Then I toss it carelessly on the table. It lands with a light thud and sticks to the glass.

Before Taylor can resume his endless squealing, I stab him in the chest. I shove it deep inside him with both hands and force my bodyweight on top of the knife. I can *feel* the life fleeing his body. It's easier to tell when their eyes remain intact, but his struggle subsides, his panic vanishes, and within half a minute, he's gone. Gone forever.

I have taken Taylor's soul for my purposes, and it will never be laid to rest. I twist the knife around and wrench it back and forth, widening the fatal wound. The blade slips out easily. I wipe it on his clothes and then place it back inside my boot.

I reach my hand inside the hole that the knife left behind. It's nearly wide enough to fit my entire fist inside now. I push past his burned skin and feel the wet tissue within. After a moment's fumbling, I touch something solid that fills my grasp. It beats no longer, but unmistakably, it is Taylor's heart.

I take it firmly in my hand and then wriggle it from his body. Gently, I pull it out, feeling my hand slip through his moist chest cavity. Once I pull his heart through the opening, I stare down at it, awestruck. I hold the glistening organ with both hands and feel a tear working its way down my cheek. Standing in the field of victory now, I am elated.

The world is swirling around me. My body feels weightless as I begin walking toward the pentagram. I lower myself onto my knees, reach my hands out, and raise the heart just below my markings. "I offer this sacrifice unto you, dear Lucifer. Guide thy servant and accept my humble offering." Generous tears flow down my cheeks as I breathe deeply. The air itself fills my chest and lungs with an all-consuming serenity.

I place Taylor's heart next to his hand on the end table. I admire my presentation for a moment before something dawns on me. *Yes, that's right.* We're not quite finished yet after all. I stand up, walk over to the table, and fetch his severed eyes and tongue. I arrange them to complete my display. The hand and the heart are at the top. The eyes are spaced apart below, and the tongue is just beneath them in the center.

I stand in awe with my hands on my hips. I cannot take my eyes off it, and I can feel myself salivating. My jaw hangs and my lips are open, but I am speechless. After a moment of prolonged admiration, I glance over at Taylor and grin. His cheeks are covered in blood; it drips from his mouth while his head hangs low. He seems even smaller than before. More insignificant.

I have accomplished my purpose here.

But still, what is life without the performance of art? More must be done. I remember that there were a few cans of paint inside his living room closet. I walk toward the door and inspect them. Five gallons of it sit upon the floor. There are assorted colors too: a ruby red, white, gray, forest green, and black.

I retrieve a screwdriver from the bag of tools and use it to open the red can of paint. Then I take the can and begin splashing its contents around the room. Its deep, rich color stains the wall above the brown sofa in his living room. I throw a little onto Taylor's inert corpse; it covers his torso and lap. Then I dump the remainder of the can onto the floor around my feet, and it makes a wonderful mess of things. I open the remaining cans of paint in the closet and repeat the process over and over again.

The entirety of Taylor's living room is now covered in lush, unsystematic color. Dense splotches of it splatter the walls and furniture; my lifeless audience cheers my efforts behind empty eyes and severed limbs. Several colors of paint drip from the table and onto the floor. I cherish it intensely, though I can't say why. But that's the nature of creation, isn't it?

I pick a paintbrush out of the bag and reapproach Taylor's body. I dab the brush onto some of the paint that's already mixed together on the table. Then I hold his head up and paint a large frown over his lips. I place the brush in his hand, bending the broken fingers as necessary to keep it in place.

Then I take a step back and close my eyes. *"Hail Satan,"* I whisper, drawing in the fresh air around me.

As much as I hate to do so, I must get going now. I've been here for nearly an hour, perhaps longer. It's hard to tell in the moment. But I can remain here no longer. I look down at myself, and for the first time, it becomes fully apparent that my clothes are drenched in his blood. And that...just won't do, will it?

I make my way to Taylor's bedroom, turn the light on, and begin searching through his closet. I find a tan Carhartt jacket and a pair of jeans. I don't bother taking off my bloody garments. It would constitute evidence, a threat to my very freedom. So instead, I just put the jacket on and wear his pants over mine. I check myself out in the mirror. "Good as new," I say, smiling, and tugging on the edges of the coat.

Now that I have everything situated, it's time for my departure. I think it's best to avoid the front door. You never know. Some nosy neighbor may have heard the sounds of my friend's demise and become suspicious enough to check things out.

I walk over to the window in the center of his bedroom, then open the blinds and peer out. It seems the coast is clear. I unlock the window and raise it open. The screen is still in place, so I push it out. Then I stick my head out the window and see no one. It's time to go.

I stick my leg out and climb onto the ground. There's some shrubbery next to the window; I crouch by it as I scan the area one last time. Paranoia. It's truly the worst part of the job. And it doesn't matter how many times I've done this, because it comes for me regardless. It works its tentacles inside your brain, and before you know it, every sound of the night raises the alarm for your expected apprehension.

But the night is still. There is a gentle breeze working its way through the air. I feel its chill upon my skin as I watch the remaining leaves tremble on their limbs. The streetlights emit a dim, sickly green light, and I am euphoric. I stick my hands in my jacket pockets and keep my head low as I pace quickly down the street, heading toward the neighborhood entrance.

It's been a striking execution, a substantial relief. I have fed my dragon for the time being. He thrives under the succor I've provided.

And this…is home.

Chapter Two

I.

Amazon Distribution Center—Atlanta, Georgia

November 15, 2024

11:15 a.m.

I'm back again. Back to the horrible, mundane realities of my everyday life. Yellow plastic containers surround me once more. And to make matters worse, today is my birthday. I reflect on my thirty-five trips around the sun and realize that each has made me worse than the last.

I am wearing my navy blue uniform, staring off, and completely consumed by my own thoughts. I lean against the guardrail with one elbow. My eyes are to the floor and my hair hangs in front of them.

The way he looked…the way he sounded. The sheer terror of that night swallows me whole as I dwell upon the memory. It's been nearly two weeks now, and I can't stop reliving it. I fantasize about the scene, about the paint covering the walls, and his scorched face—eyeless and frowning.

I need to kill again. I need to be of service and to put myself to a higher use. There's something greater than being another cog in this impotent machine. I don't care anymore; I can't even pretend to. My apathy is boundless. To hell with these packages and their many recipients. My frustration swells, and I can feel the hunger growing inside. It devours me from within as I ache for its powerful release.

It's time. It must be. The Dark Lord needs me, I can feel it. It comes as an ever-pressing aura that grows around me. A dark cloud that only I can see. It becomes denser and more definite with each passing day. And still, I must report here. I must carry on, checking, processing, and moving things along with the rest of them.

I can feel myself trembling against the guard rail, and it wakes me from my dream. I return to my station and make myself look busy, scanning the barcodes on packages, and placing them in their respective slots. My supervisor passes by with his clipboard in hand; I can feel his gaze. Pass along, simple swine. Nothing for you to see here. I am just as busy as the rest of them. Production. Creation. I am carrying my weight and doing my part.

But maybe it's time for a change. Perhaps next time it should be a woman. I've killed women before, but it's often more enjoyable to kill a man. Maybe there's just more to hate about them, or the chase is greater. Who's to say? Either way, variety is the spice of life.

II.

Downtown Atlanta Library
November 15, 2024
6:30 p.m.

And there she is, my delightful prey. She's wearing a dark red leather jacket and navy blue jeans. She has leather boots and dark brown hair. She couldn't be older than thirty. Well, maybe thirty-one. I've never been good at guessing ages.

I've been studying her for the past hour without her knowledge. I am preoccupying myself with occult literature as I gaze up at her. I'm wearing all black, from my jeans to my denim jacket and boots. She's busy working at one of the desks, concentrating underneath the faint lamplight. She scribbles notes onto a pad while referring to a book by her side.

The library is sparsely populated at this hour. The sun has already begun to set, and it seems that most readers have already left for the day. But here we are, she and I. Our fates are vastly intertwined, though she does not know it yet.

I've been smart, I think to myself. It's a different methodology. Different scouting location. Different gender. I've studied many of history's most successful killers, and that's the key takeaway: avoid patterns. They'll lead to your detection. So tonight, I will do things right. I was overeager before. I shouldn't have killed Taylor on the same night that I met him. That was sloppy; I can see that now. But the most important thing is to learn from our mistakes and not repeat them.

Another ten minutes pass. The pair of us continue busying ourselves with our cross-purposes. The librarian is dutifully taking books one by one from a little handcart; she places them back onto their respective spots on the shelf. The librarian approaches the woman and gently reminds her that the library will be closing in fifteen minutes.

The woman seems surprised by this and checks the time on her phone. She sighs and stretches her arms in the air, recovering from the day's effort. Then she begins packing her things and preparing for her departure.

After she's packed her books, notepad, and laptop, she slings her computer bag across her shoulder. She starts heading toward the entrance at a leisurely pace. I can tell that she's been here for some time, working hard, no doubt. I wait several seconds after she passes to collect my things. Then I begin my pursuit.

She's maybe twenty feet ahead of me. We're walking down a long aisle between two rows of dark wooden bookshelves. I swear, I can smell her, even from this distance. A faint trace of perfume lingers behind her, and it lures me in. It whispers an invitation inside my ear: *come closer*.

But I won't. Not yet. I must exercise control. I must be impenetrable. She smiles politely to the elderly woman working behind the front desk and then walks through the security screeners by the front door. She pushes the handle and opens it. Then something catches her attention. The woman reaches into her pocket and pulls out her phone, examining it.

Dammit. I'm right by the front desk and I can't just stop. There's nothing around to busy myself with. No displays to peruse, no items to fumble with. I slow my pace, hoping she hurries herself along. But she doesn't. She's standing in the doorway, typing something to someone. I continue advancing toward her slowly, hoping to go unnoticed.

Finally, she looks up from her phone and spots me approaching the doorway. "Sorry," she says with a playful smile. She walks through the door and holds it open for me. "No problem," I reply, smiling back at her. She turns and begins heading down the sidewalk, looking down at her phone again.

I'm frustrated. I start gritting my teeth as I watch her walk away. I'm not letting this one go, I decide. She's exactly what I'm searching for; her blithe innocence calls out to me. So, I decide to wait it out for a bit. Yes, just give her a little distance, that's the answer. I lean against the brick wall outside the library and wait.

I give her about fifteen seconds for a head start. Then I start walking, keeping my eyes fixed upon her as we go. I study my surroundings also, taking stock of the people passing me by with short, judgmental glances. She makes a left turn up ahead and starts heading into an alleyway. It makes me nervous that she's gotten out of my line of sight, so I quicken my pace slightly. Once I reach the building's corner by the alley, I peek my head out and have a look. Still there, I see.

She's walking rather slowly and seems to have no specific intent about her. A man opens one of the back doors in the alleyway and takes out the trash, but he returns inside quickly. Good. We don't need anyone observing us, do we?

We continue walking for another fifteen seconds, and she still hasn't looked behind her even once. *It would be so easy*, a little voice tells me, *to do it right here, right now.* No...I mustn't. I can't risk being seen in public. And there's always someone watching, whether you feel them there or not.

But then again...there isn't anyone. No witnesses of any kind. Only she and I dwell inside this long, desolate alleyway. And it's nearly dark. I love the winter; it feels like it's always dark.

Well, maybe it's okay, then. Yes...after all, I've been good long enough, and all that patience has begun taking its toll. I've been disheveled, disoriented—denied a single drop of blood for what feels like ages. And wouldn't this the better way to break the pattern? It could look like a mugging gone wrong, and they'll never link it to the previous murder. Can't do too many home invasions. That itself is a pattern.

The woman stops walking for a moment and types something into her cell phone. She brings it to her ear, and it seems that she's placing a call. She leans against a handrail that runs along a concrete ramp behind an Italian restaurant.

She still doesn't bother turning around. I walk a few paces toward her, closing what little distance remains between us. I crouch behind a nearby dumpster and listen in. I can hear her placing an order for Chinese food, and I'm relieved. That shouldn't matter at all. I pull a four-inch switchblade from my pocket and press the button to release the blade.

Then I stand from my place of hiding and begin taking short, silent steps toward her. My eyes are growing wide as I advance with the knife lowered by my side. I am but ten feet away when she hears the scrape of my feet against the asphalt. She turns and then stares at me with alarm.

The woman is frozen in fear. She's awestruck with her mouth hanging open. As I walk the final paces, she reaches inside her bag and pulls something out. And before I know what's happened, all I can feel is the stinging—the deep, gnawing acid crawling its way into my eyes. The selfish bitch has maced me, and now I'm stumbling in the streets like a buffoon, screaming, and clawing at my eyes to stop the burning.

But this isn't the first time I've been sprayed, and I won't let her get away that easily. I begin slashing at her wildly, waving my arm through the air with the blade in hand. She continues backing up in the alley as I pursue her. She starts digging in her bag again and pulls out a small black 9mm pistol. She points it at me and suddenly has a renewed sense of confidence about her. I've always loved a challenge.

I lunge toward her. My blade reaches its target as I catch her right hand. It makes a large incision. She drops her pistol as the blood starts flowing. I quickly kick the gun away when she attempts to pick it back up. Unable to retrieve her weapon now, she begins to run.

I stab her in the back as I pursue her. Then I place my hand on her shoulder and turn her to face me. She's pressed against the wall now. I raise my knife in the air, preparing to drive it into her chest, but then she raises an arm to block me and punches me in the gut.

As I reel from the blow, she uses her bag to knock the knife from my hand. Both items fly several feet away. I do not have time to retrieve my weapon, because now she is running away again. Her injuries barely seem to slow her down. I chase after her and grab her from behind. My eyes are still screaming in pain as I wrap my hands around her throat.

She turns, grabs my hands, and tries to pry them off, but my strength is too great, my determination too fierce. The woman rears her leg back and knees me in the groin. The pain reverberates throughout my body, and I feel sick. My hands loosen involuntarily as she escapes my grasp.

As I'm doubled over and retching, I glance up at her, full of hatred. She draws her arm back and gouges me in the eyes. I cry out in pain, then fall back and put my hands to my throbbing eyes.

I can barely see her as she pounces upon me. We fall to the ground, and she mounts herself on top of me. I buck my hips to throw her off, but she elbows me in the face. I crack her hard on the jaw, yet the force is not enough to knock her off. Wearily, she reaches behind her and grabs something. As I raise my fist to strike her again, I feel metal upon my wrist and hear the clicking sound of handcuffs being fastened.

"You gluttonous whore!" I yell. "You self-righteous bitch!"

She grabs my other arm, and we struggle against each other for a moment. She raises up and uses her elbow to strike me hard in the solar plexus. Her blood splashes onto my clothes. She manages to fasten the other hand, and I am left gasping for air after the wind has been knocked out of me.

Then I regain my focus. Frantic now, I shove her off me with my adjoined hands. She falls beside me, and I roll onto my belly. I manage to raise myself to my knees and begin staggering down the alley. She jumps to her feet and rushes over to the gun that's still lying on the pavement several feet away. She grabs it, then says, "Stop or I'll shoot!"

I glance back at her but continue hobbling away. Not today, not ever, I'm thinking. Goddammit, this is what I get for veering off plan. How could I be so *stupid?!* I hear the first shot ring out and it ricochets off a dumpster next to me. I begin moving faster. This could be it. My breath is ragged, and my heart is racing as I desperately try to reach the end of the alley. It's not far. I can make it.

She fires again. And before anything registers, I am falling to the ground. My shoulder is on fire, and I'm screaming in agony. "Curse you, heinous wretch!"

She keeps her eyes fixed upon me as I lie defenseless on the ground. I am rolling around, trying to gather the strength to lift myself up again. She retrieves her fallen bag and pulls a radio from it. She starts speaking into it, but I can hardly focus on that now, because it is time to go.

Slowly, I rise to my feet again. I fight through the pain as the world begins closing in around me. Adrenaline floods my body, and I am able to run somehow. I bolt down the alley as quickly as I can. I'm unable to swing my arms, so the handcuffs are jostling back and forth in front of me. I'm panting, sweating, and brimming with nervous energy.

I'm at the end of the alley when a middle-aged, dark-skinned man wearing a black overcoat jumps out from the corner. He's wrinkled and has messy, peppered hair and a thick mustache with stubble all around. He points his gun at me and commands me to stop. He lays a hand on me as I try to run past him. I jerk violently and use my conjoined hands like a club, knocking the silver pistol from his grip.

He tries to grab me again, this time with both arms. I'm pulling and tugging to get away from him, but it's doing me no favors. Then I lunge toward him, bringing our faces as close as I can. I bite him hard on the cheek, tasting his metallic blood upon my lips. Then I spit on the ground as it dribbles down my chin.

The man is angry now, drawing a hand to his face to wipe the spot. He punches me hard in the gut and takes hold of me once again. He's trying to force me to the ground when I rear back and headbutt him. It hurts like hell, but it seems to have done the job. The man leans down and rubs the spot on his forehead where we collided. The world is spinning now, but I have no time to waste. I turn the other way, stumble through an intersection, and begin running down the sidewalk.

I'm struggling to breathe as I continue my flight. *Fuck*, I really should put in more time at the gym. I feel a hand grasping at my shoulder behind me. I jerk, trying to throw him off me, but he grabs a fistful of my jacket and drags me down. I land in a pile of black trash bags outside of a convenience store.

A uniformed police officer is standing over me; he's young with jet-black hair. I stare at him like a caged animal. I lift my torso off the bags, but before I can make it all the way up, he begins cracking me hard with a nightstick. I roll out of the way to escape his blows. Then I fall to the ground, and he sets upon me again, crouching down to my level. He lands another blow before I draw my legs back and kick him in the stomach. The officer grunts loudly as he doubles over from the impact. I twist my body and make it up to my knees again.

Right when I think I'm in the clear, another man appears. I look up at him with scornful disappointment. *Ugh*—he has his taser drawn. The officer's face is angry and warlike as he pulls the trigger. The little metal prongs pierce my shirt and dig into my stomach. The charging, electrical pulse runs throughout my body. I am paralyzed as my muscles seize. He holds the charge for what seems like an eternity. Bees are crawling through my skin. My brain shakes inside my skull, and I lie motionless in agony.

Helpless and defeated, I can barely breathe. I watch him holster his taser. He walks over and puts a hand on his friend's shoulder. "You all right?" he asks the fellow officer.

"Yeah. I'm fucking fine," the other replies, glaring down at me. He takes a few steps toward me and clenches his jaw. Then he starts cracking me hard on the legs with his nightstick. My body twists and writhes as I try to escape his blows. But it's of no use. He moves with me, and I am too weak to stop him.

"Smith, Jefferson, cut that shit out!" a voice calls. It's the older man with the black overcoat from the alley. He's running toward us sluggishly and waving his arms in the air. "Knock it off, dumbass," he chides the officer as he approaches. "Can't have some goddamn ACLU lawyer suing our asses."

"Sorry, Detective," the man offers sheepishly. "He bought it, though." The officer returns the nightstick to his duty belt.

"Well, don't just stand there looking at me, get him up," the detective replies. He shakes his head and watches as the two uniforms help me onto my feet. My head hangs low, and my hair covers most of my eyes. I feel exhausted. I can't help but smirk a little as I notice the wound on the man's face. He eyes me up and down with disgust. The detective hears footsteps approaching behind him; he turns his head. It's the woman from the alley.

"Where the hell were you?" she asks, gesturing with annoyance. "What took you so long?"

"You didn't call for help."

"I couldn't, he knocked my bag out of my hand. That's why you were supposed to have eyes on us, remember?"

"What can I say? I'm getting too old for this shit," he offers with a slight grin.

"What happened to your face?" she questions.

His smile fades. The older detective grimaces, touching the spot on his cheek. "Crazy bastard bit me." He eyes her curiously for a moment. "What the hell happened to *you?*" he asks, nodding toward her bleeding hand.

She looks down at her dripping wound as if she's just now noticing it. "He cut me. The vest must have slowed the other one." She lifts her collar and takes stock of the blood on her shoulder and the protective vest beneath her shirt.

"Make sure somebody looks at that once EMS gets here," he tells her. She nods. The older man glances at me, then shakes his head. He points and says, "If that ain't the guy, I don't know who is."

She steps closer, sizing me up with arrogant satisfaction. "It's him, all right."

Chapter Three

I.

Fulton County Police Department

November 15, 2024

9:30 p.m.

"You're sure you're good, then?" the older detective asks.

"Yeah, I'll be fine," his partner replies. "Wasn't as bad as it looked."

"Well, take tomorrow off to be sure. It was good work today," the older detective commends her.

"I know," she answers slyly, arching her eyebrows with a half-smile.

They've adjusted my restraints, and my hands are now locked behind my back. She's leading me through the police station by the arm. Her name is Amara Cruz. The older one is Carter Murphy. I listened intently to their conversation while sitting in the back of their squad car. Unfortunately, I couldn't glean much else.

I study Amara's injuries through the corner of my eye. Her hand is wrapped in gauze. I can see a bandage protruding from her jacket's collar. I am surrounded by countless gaping cretins wearing dark blue uniforms.

45

My revulsion heightens with every new set of eyes that I meet, and I feel sick.

Carter nods. "Knew it was a good call putting you on this."

"I agree," Amara replies.

"Yeah, don't let it go to your head, though. You're still a boot to me, kid."

"Everyone's a boot to you, Carter."

"Keep your ageist remarks to yourself, young lady."

Amara laughs at his comment while she leads me toward a reinforced window. There's a fat, pale cop standing behind it; he's staring at me with a dumbfounded expression behind the thick glass. His mouth hangs open, causing his already bountiful chin to double. Amara pulls my wallet out of an evidence bag and then studies my driver's license. "We've got a Mr. Dalton Asher here," she informs the man behind the glass.

The man on the other side of the window suddenly awakens from his stupor. "What's the charge?" he asks.

"Attempted murder and aggravated assault...for now," she replies casually, keeping a firm grip on my arm.

The heaving rhinoceros on the other end grunts, scratches his nose, and says, "Hot damn. That's a big ticket."

"Sure is."

"All right, well, take him over to holding cell six for now. We'll get him processed. You got your report finished?"

"Not yet. I'll have it to you soon."

"We'll need it before his bond hearing. Make it quick."

"Always do," she replies. They smirk at one another, reveling in their shared righteousness, their duty-bound goodness.

"Come on, you," she says, tugging at my arm. She leads me through the open lobby and then down a hallway toward a row of cells. I limp along as the pain sets in from the blows to my legs. The blood from earlier has dried; it makes my clothes cling to my skin. The paramedics patched me up too when they came. I'm sure whatever glue they used will hold just long enough for them to fry me—one can only hope.

The walls are baby blue cinderblocks. In front of the cells are sliding gray doors with a single large window in the center. As we pass them by, an inmate stares curiously from each window. They're like stray dogs at supper time—dumb, empty, and hungry.

Amara looks over at a cop that's sitting behind a long desk that stretches throughout the lobby. "Detective Cruz," he greets her, stretching out each syllable. "How ya been?"

"I'm good," she replies. "Got one for cell six." The man nods and then presses a button beneath the counter. A cell door opens mechanically about twenty feet away. Amara leads me to it, and it seems that I have found my new home.

II.

Fulton County Police Department

November 17, 2024

1:00 p.m.

"I can't believe we finally got him," Amara mutters.

"Took long enough. These task forces don't normally drag on like this," Carter replies. "He was a tricky one. No fingerprints in the system. Didn't leave much of a pattern at first. Victims seemed random. Guess he got sloppy, though. They always do. They get hungry, and then they do something stupid. If he hadn't left that little calling card on the last one, we probably wouldn't have pieced it all together."

The two detectives are sitting inside a break room within the police station. The glass in the center of the door reads, "Fulton County Homicide." Each is enjoying a cup of coffee while eating their lunch. "Yeah," Amara replies, "I just hope his prints match the ones we got from the scene."

"Oh, they will," Carter replies confidently. "Looks like he wanted you pretty bad," he adds, smirking. "Not the worst thing, really. Thought I'd be retired before anybody nabbed his ass."

Amara chuckles. "So did I..."

"You're real funny, you know that?" Carter grins and shakes his head. "I'm serious, though. These last fifteen years, I've never seen a serial take this long to catch. Maybe a few did before my time, but damn..."

She stirs her coffee. "You didn't have me before."

Carter smiles and says, "Guess you did it all by yourself, then, huh?"

"I wouldn't say that..." Amara replies, taken aback by her partner's candor.

Carter stares at her flatly and then smiles. "Relax. I'm giving you a hard time. You're off to a good start here. Figuring out the whole Satanic angle, then connecting those cases together...that's how we got him. It'll help you stand out for promotions too."

She nods and stares at the table while she sips her coffee.

"You got that report ready?" he asks.

"Yeah, I looked through all my notes. Everything's in there. There's no way he'll make bail. Should be an airtight case."

"Good."

III.

Atlanta Department of Corrections

November 19, 2024

9:00 a.m.

I'm in my cell now. It's a different cell than before. When they first denied my bail, I felt a little lively. I shrieked and howled as the judge announced his resolution. The confounded cop standing next to me tried to force my compliance. He wanted to quiet me—so I bit his ear off. Well, half of it, anyway.

My boundless screeching filled the courtroom while the judge stared in awe. I spat the shredded lobe onto the ground as a few more officers came to settle me down with their batons. I yelled obscenities through bloodstained lips as they wrestled me to the ground. But this is all in the past now.

Because here I am. Alone. Angry. Vile. I sit on the cement floor next to the wall. It is a fading bronze color with numerous markings upon it; the remnants of its former inhabitants persist and tell the story of the room's occupancy. What has become of them? I wonder to myself. I make my markings alongside theirs. I scratch a large Leviathan Cross into the wall with a pen that I bought from the commissary. I take my time, making it even and pronounced. It is all I have to do, after all. There's no violence to be had, no sacrifice to offer. I must simply wait.

How could I let this happen? I've been subdued by the one I was supposed to be hunting. The wretched do-gooder. The hopeless romantic. She can solve the world's many problems with all her efforts, can't she?

But we'll always kill each other. We'll forever eat one another the moment we're hungry enough. And you can't purge hunger, can you, Detective?

She has locked me up in this horrid cell, and it seems that I may never get out—but there will always be another. And another. And plenty more after that. So bask in your victory while you can. It is transient. You'll never see the last of my kind.

I hear footsteps coming down the hall. No matter, I shall not be distracted. The fumbling of keys in front of my door does not take me from my task. A lock clicks, and the door lurches open. Two guards walk inside my cell. They're both somewhere in their mid-twenties with matching dark blue uniforms.

"Goddammit," one of them complains. He sighs and cuts his eyes toward his friend.

"Hey, we told you already...you can't write on the walls in here," the other adds angrily.

I do not look at them. I will not give them the dignity of it. I continue etching my designs onto the wall. One of them approaches and nudges me with his foot. His hands are on his hips, and he stares down at me expectantly. Go on, you buffoon, you hideous mammal. He reaches down and tries to grab the pen from my hand, but I jerk my arm away and hiss at him. I stare into his eyes with black hatred.

"Fucking freak..." he says, shifting his gaze between his friend and me.

The pair of them are hovering over me now. They're talking with their eyes to one another. They come on either side and each grabs ahold of me as I jostle against them. I scream and yell as they force my back against the wall. My body feels tight and rigid as they press me onto it. After a moment's struggle, one of them places restraints around my wrists and ankles; I feel them clicking against my flesh as they lock.

"Come on, sweetheart, it's time for your hearing," he mocks.

My heavy breathing subsides. Rage turns to sullen acceptance. I trod along the hallway with my head down. I walk between the apes; each of them maintains a loose hold on my arm. They heave and grunt as they escort me down a flight of stairs, and before long, we are inside a courtroom.

It's a different judge than before. He's young for a judge, probably somewhere in his forties with boyish brown hair. He looks at me cautiously, though I can sense his disapproval. "All right, Counselors, if you're ready, let's get started."

The bailiff forces me to sit in a chair next to a nervous looking man. I assume he's my public defender. He's younger, dark-skinned, and bald with a goatee. A decent suit, but I can tell he doesn't make much, doing what he's doing.

They tried to call me from my cell several days ago to speak to an attorney about the trial, but I'd refused. I wanted no part in it. This is all a monstrous sham. These people have no authority. Not over my body, not over my actions. I answer only to one, and he does not dwell in this land of endless hope. It's all a masquerade, a simple way of making themselves *feel* better, but it will all be to no avail.

The sounds of the room become lost in a wave of white noise. I am on another plane of existence as the courtroom voices begin their hushed exchanges. The world is washed over in an awful shade of pure white, and I am enveloped. It is a tidal wave that paints over everything in its path. Time and space elude me as I stare helplessly into the colorless void that it creates. I have no idea how long it's been: how long I've been here, how long these people have been talking, how long since my last kill.

My mind continues racing. Paranoia infiltrates my thoughts. My teeth are chattering, and my leg shakes as I stare into the burning sun. But just as suddenly as it came, the light vanishes. The world grows quite dim while a vision consumes me.

Alone and naked now in the nighttime desert, I'm waiting on something to happen. I'm not sure what. I'm seated on the rocky ground, perched up with my hands behind me. It feels like I've been here for ages, like I was born here. Nothing but red craggy rock and stone hills surround me. The moon is full and bright, but not a single star shines in the pitch-black sky.

I hear something shifting. The earth itself begins to quake gently. Then it escalates. Pulsing vibrations give way to cracking topsoil. A chasm appears and then starts to widen. It becomes large. I stand to my feet for fear that it will spread and swallow me inside its chaos.

My breath quickens. I'm not frozen with fright, but I cannot force myself to look away, either. I cannot run. Rock and soil flood into the opening hole; it cascades down the side in an avalanche that pours into nothing.

Closer and closer, the falling ground approaches. I'm looking into the endless hole in the earth beneath me. I take a startled step back when it suddenly appears to stop. Stray rocks continue tumbling down the walls, but the hole is no longer swallowing the earth.

I hear only the sound of the dry desert breeze. It clutches my neck, and I feel a chill run down my spine. I'm suddenly self-aware. Questions race through my mind quicker than I can process them.

An awful sound comes from the depths of the cavern. It grows louder as something like a freight train works its way up from below. I can see its dreadful head and eyes emerge from the darkness as I stand over the open hole, staring in amazement.

I'm speechless and cannot cry out at all. A black form emerges from the hole and then shoots out into the sky. Its body is larger than a building. A proud serpent hovers above me now, staring decisively while it continues stretching itself overhead. Its scales glimmer in the ample moonlight. Acid drips from its forked tongue while it flicks in the air, and a wide hood flanks both sides of its head.

The snake begins lowering itself down to my level. It cranes its mighty neck toward me. The mouth of the hideous serpent draws nearer while I stand with my feet firmly entrenched. My fists are balled and my eyes are peeled as storm clouds gather in the distance.

Blue smoke trails from the base of the earth's opening. I feel the first drops of rain come when the titanic serpent stops just before me. Its head is the size of a bus. The menacing black eyes pierce into me as I stand in awe of it. It's mere feet away now, and I can reach out and touch it if I want to.

IV.

Fulton County Superior Court
November 19, 2024
10:30 a.m.

"How dare you?!" I scream at the top of my lungs, banging on the table with my shackled hands.

The courtroom falls silent. The judge is taken aback, staring at me with confusion. "Counselor, please advise your client to keep quiet during these proceedings," he warns.

I breathe heavily but regain my composure. I can feel my chest rising and falling as the fire inside fades to an ember. Many words have been said; I can see that now. The room's dynamic is somehow different. Something has happened here.

As I'm starting to piece together all the puzzle's parts, the judge reaches for his gavel. "Given the evidence presented, I find that there is probable cause to proceed to trial. The defendant will be remanded to the State's custody for the duration of these proceedings." He bangs the gavel against his desk, and I am only left to wonder what all of this means.

It seems they've taken my freedom. That's all that really matters, I suppose. My attorney is standing next to me now, and I tug at his sleeve. He looks down at me and warns me to stop with his eyes while he shakes his head.

A few more formalities are exchanged, and before I know it, the bailiff approaches me. He takes hold of my arm and then helps me onto my feet. I am forced to take short, choppy steps with my hands and feet cuffed together as he escorts me from the courtroom. Before long, I'm led back to my cell in a fog of dense smoke.

V.

Fulton County Superior Court

December 9, 2024

1:00 p.m.

The trial has begun. It started some time ago, several weeks past, I think. They've medicated me on something to calm me down, to inhibit me. But they'll never break me. They'll never silence my voice nor impede my mission. We are violence that cannot be quelled.

They've brought in countless exhibits. We've seen several photographs and artifacts already. The witnesses and experts have proffered their testimony. My attention wanes as the process drags on.

I loathe the prosecutor. I detest everything about him. His polished arrogance is boundless. The man has been scurrying around this courtroom, for segment after segment, gesturing wildly with his hands. He points at me and tells the polite jury what a bad boy I've been. He radiates trite virtue. His eyes are judgment, and his voice is condemnation.

His name is Henry Adams, though I've heard others call him Hank. He's the prosecuting attorney for the State of Georgia. I assume he comes from a long line of lawyers and important people. He appears every day, well dressed and groomed. His dirty blonde hair is always swept to the side, and it never seems to move. He's made himself a symbol. His pure obstinance in the pursuit of justice has earned him respect from his colleagues, the community. But what do they know? They're merely here for the show. They stuff their greedy mouths while he doles out undeserved demise.

I've seen him before on television. The news is always on inside the rec room. Those faint glimpses have shown me who this man is; I have witnessed his inner being. And now, this...charlatan, this misguided hack is trying to upend all that I've worked for. I can see him swaying the jury's minds; he's causing their gears to turn in his favor. His little presentation isn't over yet, but things aren't going well for me.

"Your Honor, for our next witness, the State would like to call Mollie Hamilton," Henry tells him. The young prosecutor turns his head and watches as one of my alleged victims makes her way to the stand. She's short, razor-thin, and has messy teal hair. She stinks of death. Little Mollie Hamilton. She wears an eyepatch, and the word "Pig" is scarred into her cheek, a fun reminder of our time together. She was one of my very first exploits here—the one who got away. I must say, this wasn't my best work.

Mollie makes her way nervously to the podium. She refuses to look at me as she walks past. Judge Erickson is an older, stout man. He'll be presiding over the rest of my case. His white hair is slicked back neatly. I'd put him around sixty-five.

Judge Erickson has Mollie stop just before entering the stand. She raises her right hand as the elderly judge swears her in. She gives a solemn oath and promises to tell the truth. After she's seated, Henry starts by asking her a few preliminary questions. Where she lives, what she does for a living. It's all a tedious drudgery, watching this.

"Can you tell the jury where you were on the evening of March 24th?" Henry questions.

"Yes. I was on my way home from a nightclub," she begins. "I'd been out with a group of girls. We were celebrating my friend's birthday. The whole night...it felt like this guy was watching me, just staring at me from across the room. Not in a good way, either. There was something off about him, like he wanted to hurt me."

"I had a few drinks at the club, and I wasn't feeling right about being there anymore. I wanted to go home. I asked a few of my girlfriends if they wanted to go with me, but I couldn't convince them to leave. I told them how I felt, but they just said he looked harmless. Like some creep looking to get laid. But I knew I didn't want to be there any longer than I had to."

"So, I headed outside and started scrolling through my phone. I was going to get an Uber. I checked my bank account first and saw that I was pretty broke. I only had about $50 in my checking at the time. I felt nervous about it, but I couldn't afford the ride home. I didn't live far, so I decided to walk."

"I headed down the sidewalk and tried to stay in well-lit areas...But I could feel him there. I know he was following me."

"Objection, Your Honor, the witness is speculating," my attorney interrupts.

Old man Erickson tilts his head for a moment. He looks to the prosecutor before replying, "Sustained. The jury will disregard the witness' last comment. Ms. Hamilton, please keep your testimony limited to the events you actually observed."

Mollie nods her head somewhat nervously and looks down into the witness stand. "I walked quickly. I just wanted to get back as fast as I could. About fifteen minutes later, I made it home. Everything was all right, and I felt relieved. I made sure my front door was locked, then I drew myself a bath."

"I took my time and relaxed. I...I must have started falling asleep. Because when I opened my eyes, I saw him standing over me," she says, pointing a shaky finger in my direction.

"Let the record show that Ms. Hamilton has identified the defendant, Dalton Asher, as her assailant," he replies flatly, looking to the court reporter. "How could you tell it was him?"

"He had the exact same build as the guy from the club. His outfit was the same too. He was wearing a ski mask when I first saw him, but he took it off later."

"I see. Please continue," the prosecutor responds with a gentle nod. Just when I thought I couldn't hate him any more, the loathsome slime.

"The second I opened my eyes, I panicked. I tried to get out of the tub as quickly as I could, but it was slippery inside. When I got to my feet, I hit my knee on the edge and fell on the floor. He just...stood there the whole time with his hands on his hips, staring at me. I could see his smile through the mask."

I can feel myself beginning to salivate as she recounts the tale. I wish I'd finished her that night, but it's almost worth it to hear the miserable bitch have to relive it all while the jury grimaces. They squirm in their seats as she tells them all about how I bound her hands and threw her on the bed. How I held her down and cut those three letters into her cheek. How she begged. How she sobbed. The details are so rich and entrancing. The marvelous chaos of it all comes flooding back to me through still frames and snippets of memory.

I yearn for that night. Something aches in my soul as I reflect upon it. Ah, but now she's getting to the bad part. The part where I'm pillaging through her closet, looking for instruments of mayhem and death. Yes, it's the part where she's able to break free of her bondage, and she eludes my grasp while I chase her to the front door.

I can recall it as if it were yesterday. It was the strangest feeling, standing there in her apartment after she'd fled. It was as if I owned the place now, like she'd left it all to me. I remember bellowing with laughter at the thought of it while I stood there covered in her blood, leaning against the door frame. But there was no time to dwell on such pleasantries. I thought about chasing her down and gutting her in the street like a wild hog. But I knew I had to abscond immediately. Someone would have heard us, seen us. And before I knew it, I'd be surrounded by cops; they'd gun me down and earn a medal for their heroics.

"And you're positive that you can identify the defendant as the man you encountered that night?" Henry asks, breaking my train of thought.

"I'll never forget his face...I can see him every night when I close my eyes," she says, her voice quivering. Her eyes water as she nods her pitiful head. "Yes, it was the defendant. Dalton Asher was the man I saw that night...he, he held me down and did this to me." She wipes a tear from her cheek with her left hand and then looks away. Her humiliation and embarrassment bring me some sense of relief, and I can't help but laugh aloud at her complete shame. The room falls silent when I do so, and a dozen angry, judgmental eyes fall upon me in unison.

The prosecutor's rhythm is thrown off by my short laughter, and it breaks the somber mood of the room. He looks back at me, confounded. "Uh, Your Honor, the people would like to submit exhibit twelve," he says, turning toward the judge. He hands him a small stack of papers. "It's the forensic report establishing that the defendant's fingerprints were found at Ms. Hamilton's apartment following this incident."

Several of the jurors look surprised by this. A few of them gape openly with disgust. They're getting their sick, twisted jollies as they imagine it all.

They're horrified, I can see it, but they can't manage to look away. They cannot erase this image from their minds, and part of them doesn't want to. It will be with them forever, a little piece of me dwelling in their soft, gray matter.

VI.

Fulton County Superior Court

December 10, 2024

10:00 a.m.

"If you're ready, Counselors, I'll take your closing statements," Judge Erickson says.

My lawyer approaches the jury box with his hat practically in hand. He speaks to them about the burden of proof. How I am to be presumed innocent. How the State bears the burden of proving me guilty beyond a reasonable doubt. He pokes little holes in the stories of the victims. He casts doubt upon my whereabouts on the evenings in question. He even suggests clever little alternatives to their impressionable minds. But the man knows that he is standing aboard a sinking ship. I can see it in his gestures, his nearly pleading eyes.

After my lawyer is finished, he takes his seat next to me. He seems relieved. It's as though he's done something awful and must keep it a secret. The jury looks upon him with disapproval. He wipes his brow as the prosecutor stands from his seat.

Smooth-talking Hank approaches the jury box next. He rests his hands atop the outer frame and looks down, then takes a deep breath, focusing his mind. "Ladies and gentlemen, it is not every day that I say this, but in this courtroom, we are dealing with an absolute monster, a true blight upon our community."

"Dalton Asher," he goes on, "is a man who has not shown a single shred of remorse for any of his victims. You've heard testimony from the sole survivor of his carnage. Ms. Hamilton's harrowing tale paints a portrait of the entire horrific evening. A deranged madman stalked her, bound her hands, and tortured her before she barely escaped with her life. And you've heard her positively ID *this* man as her attacker," he says, pointing perdition with his angry finger.

"The photographs of the victims tell their stories," Henry continues. He hands them an array of photographs one by one. The prosecutor observes the jury's sullen disgust as they review each of them in turn.

For the entire trial, my precious artwork has been on display for all to see, though not one has the mind to comprehend it. They've seen these pictures before, but they cannot help but revisit every detail. I can see them imagining what it must have been like. They wrinkle their brows and their stomachs churn at the sight of them.

"You've seen the forensic evidence establishing his presence at virtually every one of his crime scenes. You've heard his paper-thin alibis. And just in this courtroom today, you've heard the man himself *laughing* while his horrendous acts have been retold." He cuts his disapproving eyes toward me and scowls; an atmosphere of scathing rebuke floods the courtroom.

I can see him winning them over. They're practically shaking their little heads in unison, like silent drones following the queen bee to the inner hive. The unanimity is overwhelming. "You've heard about the rigorous investigation conducted by the police," Henry continues. "Detectives Amara Cruz and Carter Murphy have devoted themselves solely to this matter for months. Their dedication finally brought results when they landed on Dalton Asher as their primary suspect." I glance over at the detectives. They're practically gleaming as they sit upright in their seats; their posture exudes well-placed trust and singular perseverance.

"After following Mr. Asher for several weeks, they launched a successful sting operation against him. An operation which concluded in Mr. Asher attempting to stab Detective Cruz to death in a public alleyway," he says, pointing at me. He pauses and shakes his head before straightening his tie.

Henry takes a few paces away from the jury box. "He attacked several police officers as they tried to subdue him," he goes on. "It is not often that we can say with absolute certainty that a defendant committed the crimes that they're accused of. But in this case, we've caught him red-handed. We've proven his guilt beyond *any* doubt. And it is for that reason that you must find Dalton Lee Asher guilty on all charges."

He lets his words hang in the air, and the jury reflects upon them, taking in his somber expression and commanding tone. Henry heads back to his table and takes a seat. He radiates just confidence after performing his solemn duty.

Chapter Four

I.

Fulton County Superior Court

December 13, 2024

12:00 p.m.

"Mr. Edwards, I understand that the jury has reached a verdict," Judge Erickson says, tilting his head up, and looking down at the foreman.

Another day, another hearing. Though I suspect this will be the last of them. The jury deliberated for several days as I awaited their resolution in my cell. And now, it seems the farcical, moronic pool has made its final decision.

The foreman stands up. His name is James Edwards. He's white, somewhere in his mid-forties, with curly, dark brown hair. He's wearing a checkered button-up shirt with the sleeves rolled halfway. His face is hard as stone. James pushes his glasses to his face and begins reading aloud nervously. "We have, Your Honor. On the charges of murder in the first degree, we find the defendant guilty. On the charges of attempted murder, we find the defendant guilty. On the multiple counts of aggravated assault, we find the defendant guilty. And on the multiple counts of breaking and entering, we find the defendant guilty."

My agitation grows as my eyes drill small holes into the man's forehead. They are wide, bulging, and bloodshot. My knee shakes under the table as I grip the corner tightly and grit my teeth. My jaw clenches as the veins in my forehead protrude. I want his death. I want their collective agony so badly that it hurts.

I'd bind them all in chairs, sitting them in a line as I ran past them with a chainsaw. I'd run the blade across each of their bellies as I made my way to the end of the line. Their stomachs and entrails would seep onto the floor and pool together in a ceaseless swamp of humanity. I'd sever their limbs in their final moments as they looked upon their insides, spilled on the floor beneath them. And as all life drained from their impotent flesh, I'd sever their heads and kick them around the room.

I bring myself back from my fantasy and realize that the foreman has retaken his seat. The judge is staring directly at me. His pockmarked face is somber and severe. He sighs deeply before speaking in a low tone. "Dalton Asher, you have been found guilty of multiple capital offenses. Due to the nature and severity of these crimes, we will hold a separate hearing for sentencing in the coming weeks. In the state of Georgia, the range of punishment could include up to life in prison or death. Do you have any statements that you'd like to make at this time?"

The eyes of the entire world fall upon me. Each of them is a dagger that pierces my flesh. I know what he wants me to tell them. He wants me to weep aloud and say, "I'm just so awful. I'm a *bad, bad man*. And all those poor, innocent people that I harmed...I'd take it all back if I could! Can you ever forgive me?"

But I won't. I will not give them the satisfaction—for I regret nothing. My only sorrow is that their suffering was cut short and that I could not flay *more* of them alive. They deserved it. Just like all of you staring daggers into me now deserve it. I will not apologize. I will not atone. My only offense was being caught by lesser beings.

I stand up from my seat. My clanking shackles are the only sounds filling the courtroom. My head hangs low, and my long dark hair obscures my eyes as I stare down at the table. I stand for several seconds in silence. The tension grows as the spectators await my response.

I look around the room, studying each of their faces individually. "Though our great serpent was cast to shadows, he has never fallen," I begin quietly in a murmur. "Be cautious, be vigilant, because your enemy walks among you like a roaring lion," I warn as I stand proudly with my shoulders high. The judge, the jury, the lawyers—they all stare in disbelief as my voice grows louder. "You will never be safe."

A few seconds of silence stifles the air in the room as the many onlookers consume my words. I look around, staring angrily at each of them as they avoid my gaze. "All right, Mr. Asher, I believe that'll be it," the judge interrupts. He tilts his head up and looks down his nose at me.

Judge Erickson draws a deep breath through his nostrils and expects me to capitulate to his position, to bow to his stature. I smirk back at him, telling him with my eyes that I will not. I refuse. Your black robe means nothing to me, and you are bereft of any authority whatsoever, old man.

I turn and face the gallery behind me. Several of the people seated there begin shifting in their seats and staring at me with curious eyes. "Bailiff," Judge Erickson commands, pointing at me with two fingers. The tired, overweight officer straightens from his position near the judge's podium and begins approaching me. I glance over my shoulder as he walks toward me. He's middle-aged with a short flattop, thin framed glasses, and a neatly trimmed mustache. He means business, I can tell.

He places a hand on my shoulder as I stare emptily into the crowded gallery. "You'll all taste famine and death. There'll be no sanctuary—and God will forsake you in the end."

The man puts greater pressure on my shoulder and tries forcing me to sit down. I fight against him. When he realizes that I will not be seated, he grabs me with both arms and tries wrestling me to the ground. He forces me down to one knee, and I lower my head to my chest. I drive up hard with my legs and headbutt him under his chin. The impact knocks him flat on his back, and he rolls around, dazed.

The courtroom begins clamoring. "Hey, get someone else in here now!" Judge Erickson orders. A startled observer in the back of the gallery flees the courtroom. People start standing from their seats in the back to get a better look.

I am a wild animal, and I can taste his blood in the water. I am giddy and enthralled as I throw myself upon the bailiff. He tries pushing me off but is unable. I use my chains to choke him. The veins bulge in his head as he struggles against me. Another bailiff enters the room, throwing the doors open with great urgency. The tall, bald officer runs down the aisle with his nightstick in hand.

I can hear him coming, and it forces me to draw myself away from my intended kill. I glance over my shoulder and can see that he's coming fast. I move my hands down to the bailiff's belt and unholster his service weapon. He reaches out and grabs hold of my arm, trying to prevent my destiny.

The second man is upon me now, and he starts cracking me hard on the back of my head and shoulder blades.

But it doesn't matter. Because I've managed to switch off the pistol's safety, and I fire it three times into Mr. Flattop's ribcage. He yelps in between the bursts, but you can't hear them, because it all happens so quickly, and the sound of gunfire fills the crowded room.

The bald bailiff's jaw hangs open as he stares in surprise. Instinct and training overtake him, and he steps back as he draws his service weapon. I roll onto my side quickly and fire three times upon him. I catch him twice in the stomach. He fires back at me twice as the impact jars him.

The man's shots miss, and one of them strikes an elderly juror behind me. She's bleeding from the chest and gasping for air as those around her duck beneath the panel. A female juror next to her screams and tries to help the woman as she seeks cover. But the elderly victim is a frozen lump of flesh in her chair; she's bleeding and staring up at the ceiling as she struggles to breathe.

The bailiff falls to one knee and tries to raise his pistol. But he's too weak, too diminished. I lift myself from the floor and fire on him again. He drops the pistol and faceplants as I stare down at him, wide-eyed and cackling.

The judge has risen from his seat and is taking flight from the courtroom; he's heading toward his own private exit. I spot him rushing for the door out of the corner of my eye. The shackles force me to keep my hands low, but I turn and raise the pistol as high as I can. As I have him in my sights, I hear a shot ring out behind me. I jolt forward as the bullet tears through my right shoulder.

I scream and howl as the pain rings throughout my body. I grit my teeth while I watch the little rat escape. My head cocks hard to the left as I search for my assailant. My eyes scour the courtroom quickly, and of course, it is she...the temptation who brought me here.

Amara stares at me with a face full of concern as she examines the unmitigated disaster unfolding before her. She stands in a merlot leather jacket and dark jeans, aiming her pistol at me. Her partner does the same. I try to aim my pistol back at them, but I fall to the floor before I am able. I drop the gun, and it clatters on the ground next to me.

Once Amara and Carter can see that I am subdued, they each move in. They have their pistols trained on me as they advance cautiously. I am face down on the ground and having great difficulty breathing. I lift my head up slightly, and suddenly, it weighs two hundred pounds. I extend my weary arm forward, struggling to reach for the pistol. My spindly fingers strain toward it, but before I can take the gun in my hand, Amara rushes toward me and kicks it away.

I look up at her, defeated. "You, you goddamned..." Ugh, it is entirely useless. I allow my head to collapse, resting my forehead against the ground as I gnash my teeth. I wait for it. I know that it's coming.

I feel both detectives pulling against my arms, and before I know it, they've raised me to my feet again. I'm in between them now, with each grabbing me firmly by the arm. Blood soaks through my orange jumpsuit and pools near the wound.

Reality sets in once more, and vitriolic hatred surges into my brain. "I'll kill you all!" I shriek as I push against them and try to escape their grasp.

I shove Amara hard. She loses her balance, and I'm able to break my arm free from her grasp. As I begin pushing against Carter, Amara charges back and thumps me hard on the skull with the bottom of her pistol's grip. The painful blow rings throughout my head, and my vision becomes hazy as I stumble to the ground. They both continue hitting me in fretful hysterics until I lose consciousness.

Once I'm incapacitated, they begin dragging my inert body into the hallway. All the people seated in the gallery stare in shock as I move past them. Once we reach the double doors at the end, the officers begin calling for help. More uniforms come to assist, and before I regain consciousness, an ambulance arrives.

My eyes begin to flutter. Groggily, they open. I take in the new scenery unfolding around me. I'm too weak to fight, too tired to speak. They force me into the ambulance and then strap me down once I'm inside. The detectives ride along with me while the paramedic begins tending to my shoulder. He's administering something to calm me down at Amara's request. My world becomes hazy again, and I fall into an intense, sickly-sweet slumber.

II.

Atlanta Department of Corrections

January 2, 2025

12:00 p.m.

For weeks, I have lain in this hospital bed, drifting. Time was suspended as the horrid, white clouds whisked me away. The nearly constant supply of painkillers and morphine made it all a dreamlike fantasy, a bitter non-reality.

I could not summon the strength to do anything. And even if I could, I was handcuffed to the plastic rails. An officer was with me at all times. I'd catch them staring with morbid curiosity, or they'd act as if I wasn't even there, like they were simply guarding the room itself as they filled out their reports or read the news on their phones.

Once I recuperated, they brought in a contraption. It was a dolly for my transportation. It had thick leather straps on it and little wheels at the bottom. And it came with a mask! It was made of leather too and had thin metal bars in front of the mouth. They've *learned*.

Two police officers came and hoisted me from my bed, stood me on the dolly, and then strapped me down. They placed the mask on my face, and away we went. Within an hour, we arrived at the courthouse.

And now, they're bringing me in to see Judge Erickson again. The jury is still here, but they've limited access to the gallery due to my recent theatrics. Of course, my dear friends, the detectives, are present as well. They're excited to see me, I can tell. I give them big eyes and a wide smile as I'm being wheeled past them.

They park my dolly next to a table. My defense attorney is already seated. He looks at me uncertainly. The judge waits a moment for the courtroom to fall into silence. He gives a well-rehearsed speech, though I find it a bit boring and meandering. He talks a lot about the severity of my offenses, the harm to my victims, and the danger that I present to the community. I wait patiently for him to finish.

The old man stares at me with deep, somber eyes. "It is not lightly that I have arrived at this conclusion, young man," he begins slowly. "But given that you've been found guilty of multiple capital offenses as well as the expert testimony which indicates that you are likely beyond rehabilitation, the sentence issued by this court is that you will be taken from here, back to the place from whence you came. There, you will be kept in close confinement until January 20th, 2025. And upon that date, you will be taken to the place of execution where you will receive a lethal dose of potassium chloride until you are dead. May God have mercy upon your soul."

I don't say anything. What use are my words here? I am bound and confined. In silence, I accept my sentence. Within moments, the officers wheel me out of the courtroom and take me home.

III.

Atlanta Department of Corrections

January 20, 2025

8:00 p.m.

And now, I wait for the end. I can't help but ruminate on where it all went wrong. Was it sloppiness? Greed? I knew what I was doing, that's for sure. But mistakes were made. That much is undeniable. The weight of my failure hangs around my neck, and I've brooded on it incessantly these last few weeks.

I got away with it for a long time—not just in this city, but in others as well. The sparse comfort that I still possess comes from the memory of my victims. Truth be told, I can't recall all their faces. Not as clearly as I'd like to, anyway. I can't remember many of their names, because once you do this long enough, they all gradually mesh together. They form a nameless corpse, a collective pair of eyes staring at you with empty dread.

Nonetheless, their profound suffering is something that will never leave me. Those brief snippets are the sweetest moments of my life; they've brought me here and defined my essence. They are photographs in my mind that keep me company here in my cell. The law cannot take that away. Not now, not ever. They're *mine*.

I'm not sure of an exact number. Thirty? Forty? There's really no way to know. I stopped keeping count years ago. Obviously, the police don't know about them all—certainly not about the murders in other states. They haven't even scratched the surface. They've convicted me on a small percentage of them—the ones where I made mistakes. I couldn't resist the chance to leave a few calling cards, and now that's done me in. Patterns.

Motive. Predisposition. These things are the ruby red blood that has drawn the sharks into my waters.

Goddamn them. Goddamn them all. They've hunted me like a pack of hungry dogs. These conspirators, they have chewed on the flesh of my work until there was nothing left, no room to breathe. And now that the meat is gone, they insist on consuming my bones as well.

The moon is bright as I stare out the window and watch the rain as it patters against the ground outside. The wind blows and it shakes the trees. My rambling thoughts are interrupted by the familiar buzzing of the electronic lock. A guard approaches. His keys jingle as he fiddles with the secondary lock. It clicks open, and he walks inside, carrying a tray.

"Your last meal, Asher," he reports. There's no emotion behind his words; he'll be glad when I go. I don't take my eyes away from the outside scenery. The guard stands there for a moment longer before setting the tray down and leaving the room.

A few seconds after I hear him lock the door again, I turn and examine the tray. It's not the usual stuff. No, it's steak, real steak. Fresh mashed potatoes and vegetables. I'm so glad that I'll be well nourished for my final departure.

I pick up the tray and then hold the dripping meat up close to my face. It dangles there in front of me as I examine it. I walk over to the nearest corner and sit down. Then I bring my legs in close to my chest and slouch against the wall. I begin gnawing on the steak like a paranoid rat.

It's delicious, I must admit. Better than anything I've had since I've been incarcerated. But it is not enough to overcome my general feeling of repugnance. This wretched, diseased society has beaten me. They're convinced by their own mantras, their own higher *good*. But where is it?

The rest of the world is just as black as me; they simply find ways to dress themselves up as something else. At least my work is honest. My mission is incorruptible; it has never needed pretensions nor any vague sense of morality. It carries its own weight.

This dejected feeling of helplessness begins to overwhelm me as I start chewing faster and faster. Saliva runs down the corners of my mouth as I stare emptily into the wall. My thoughts are elusive, yet they continue to torment me.

A sudden flash of lightning rouses me from my stupor. Inspiration strikes as I look to the window above and take in the ample blue light filling the night sky. "Nyaaahhh!" I scream as I throw my tray against the wall. It clangs loudly against the brick as its contents begin dripping down.

I jump to my feet with great energy. Something is surging through me, I can feel it. I stare into the mashed potatoes that have splattered onto the wall in front of me. My eyes are bulging with intensity; it's as though the powerful essence coming from within is going to force them through my skull. Animalistic hunger has taken free rein. I grit my teeth as it works its way deeper inside.

I walk over to the window, stand directly in its center, and examine the night scene below. I stand waiting until a silent voice whispers something in my ear. It quells my internal doubts and informs me that *nothing* will stop my objective. I am the incurable; I will not be corrupted; I will not be governed. You may take my bones and my flesh, but I will persist, nonetheless.

The wind is practically howling outside. The large trees out front strain under its magnificent pressure. The rain is coming in sideways as it begins flooding the lawn. The clouds above seem dense and impossibly dark.

Lightning strikes again, this time much nearer. It practically cuts one of the trees in half as one of its large limbs comes tumbling to the earth below.

Now isn't the time to lament the ruins of this enterprise. *No*, my task has merely begun. That much is clear. I fall to my knees and tilt my head to my chest. My dark curly hair hangs in front of my eyes. I'm breathing so hard that it forces my shoulders up and down in a strange, shaky rhythm. My jaw hangs low, and my eyes are opened wide.

"Proud serpent, bestow your strength upon me," I whisper, bringing my hands in close to my chest. Lightning flashes again. It's so close. It will electrify this man-made prison and set me free. The thunder roars loudly as the rain patters heavily against the window. I look up and stare at the scene in wonder.

"Fail me not, dear Lucifer. Empower thy servant to commit thy deeds," I continue. The strength of the natural world flows through me. I am empowered by elements I've never felt before. They work their way in from the building's exterior and course directly into my veins.

I begin speaking in tongues. The words flow effortlessly, but I know not what they mean. My eyes roll into the back of my head as the storm intensifies. My body becomes rigid. My arms are hyper-extended to the sides, and my neck is forced back so far that it feels like my head will touch my spine.

"Give me your command, O Dark Lord. Unleash thy terror so that I may live again!" I bellow before lowering my head again. Then I drop my arms, stand up, and place my hands upon the windowsill. I study the storm, taking in its immense power. My eyes are burning coals as the fire spreads within.

After the surge passes, a sense of calm overtakes me. It's true serenity—a peace I've never felt before. It works its way into my brain, and I am helpless toward the onslaught. I begin laughing, giggling really as it comes inside. *Yes*...I have been fed, nurtured. He will not lead me astray.

It's as though I am having an out-of-body experience. I can see the mechanisms of my body in motion. My vision remains the same. But something else is controlling me, and I am enthralled by the prospect. I move away from the window, and my body glides across the floor. It feels as if my feet are not touching the ground, the way I move about so effortlessly.

I make my way over to the bed and sit down. Then I press my back against the wall and bring my knees up to my sternum. I'm wide-eyed and smiling, breathing so deeply that entire clouds are filling my lungs. I rock back and forth against the wall as the wave of comfort washes over me in pure jubilation. Gradually, my eyelids become heavy, and I fall into the deepest, heaviest sleep that I have ever known.

IV.

Atlanta Department of Corrections

January 20, 2025

11:00 p.m.

"It's about time," Amara mutters. "Thought we'd never get here."

Carter looks at her and grins. "It ain't nothing special. One minute he's here, and the next...he's not." The pair of them are sitting inside of an old cell that has been fashioned into a waiting room. Large windows cast dim light into the dingy room with red cinderblock walls.

"Yeah, but I'll feel better knowing he's got what's coming to him," Amara replies.

Carter looks away from her and begins scrolling through his phone. "You and me both," he replies coolly.

She watches him for a moment and wrinkles her nose. "How can you be so...calm about this? It doesn't bother you anymore?"

"Not really."

She uncrosses her legs and leans back against the table that's affixed to the wall. "Or maybe you're just checked out," she challenges.

Carter doesn't bother looking up from his phone. "Hey, now...you give this job another fifteen years, and we'll see how you feel." He cuts his eyes toward her, and Amara gives a half-smile while she shakes her head.

Carter puts his phone in his pocket and leans against the table too, placing his elbows upon the rusted metal. "Look, kid...this isn't your fault. I know you want it to be. I was the same way. You just think, 'if I'd only killed him when I had the chance,' or 'I should have just caught him a little sooner...' But the fact is, you didn't. You couldn't. And that's the job. You start taking this shit home, it'll wreck your life. And *then* it's like they win."

Amara stares at the ground for a moment, taking in what Carter's told her. She sighs and looks off to the distance. "Yeah...might be a few people who disagree, though."

"It was your work that brought him in, right?"

She nods her head reluctantly.

"And you risked your ass in that alley, *right?*" He pauses there and lets his words resonate for a few seconds. "So, what else could you do, really? Been a little quicker on the draw? Took another shot and risk hitting a bystander? Nah, I don't think so. You did what you could. The man's just nuts, that's all."

Amara continues looking away. She's fidgeting with her hand when a loud buzzing sound suddenly fills the room. An electronic lock clicks open. Henry Adams and two guards step inside the long corridor. They walk a short distance to the room where Carter and Amara are seated. The ADA is dressed sharply in a pinstripe suit with a red tie. He's calm, exuding self-assurance behind his placid smile. It's his big moment before the final game. "You ready?" he asks, glancing between the two detectives.

V.

Atlanta Department of Corrections

January 20, 2025

11:30 p.m.

Carter, Amara, Henry, and the two guards walk down a sparsely lit hallway. They stride along with slow, solemn purpose. At the end of the narrow walkway, a man stands outside the last remaining door. He's wearing a gray, checkered suit. His messy hair is dark with large patches of white on each side. With his notepad in hand, the man scratches his fat nose and clears his nostrils. He wrinkles his bushy eyebrows as the five of them approach.

"Hank, we've got to stop meeting like this," the man says with a sly half-smile.

"Indeed," Henry replies.

"Say, I was wondering, could you answer me something?"

"Probably depends on what the question is."

The man grins and tilts his head. "Would you care to comment on your boss' increased use of the death penalty in capital cases? The number of inmates on death row hasn't been this high in Atlanta for decades. Seems like a re-election ploy to me."

Henry smirks, doing his best to feign civility. "I don't make policy," he tells him. "But I don't think many folks in Atlanta are going to be shedding a tear for Dalton Lee Asher."

The man's grin fades while he sizes up the district attorney. "I'll take that as a no comment," he says.

"You should. You're here to take notes, Jeff. I don't know why they let you people into these things, anyway."

Jeff smiles and unwraps a stick of gum. "Very well, Counselor. Shall we?" he asks, motioning to the open door.

"Let's," Henry replies, raising his eyebrows. Then he walks through the doorway. Several others are already seated inside. Henry surveys the somewhat crowded room and takes them all in: Judge Erickson, two members of the jury, a few prison personnel, and the survivor, Mollie Hamilton.

It's not a very large room. It has three rows of chairs, gray cinderblock walls, a bulletin board, and a large window through which the audience will view my demise. Mollie is seated in the first row by herself. She fidgets nervously and averts her eyes as the rest of them enter. She's taken to wearing her hair down now, an apparent attempt to hide the scar on her cheek.

Judge Erickson's expression is sober and cold as he nods from the center of the second row. The two jurors are seated on the far right side of the third row, chatting quietly with one another. They stop talking as they watch the others file in.

The air is thick and heavy with emotion. Henry walks in and takes a seat next to Judge Erickson. They acknowledge each other politely. The two detectives make their way to the final row on the left-hand side. Carter smiles cautiously at the two jurors seated down the row. He reaches into his jacket pocket and coughs a few times into a white handkerchief.

The room is filled with muted chatter once again. Carter leans in close to Amara's ear. "It's a shame what's happened to her," he whispers, nodding toward Mollie in the front row.

"What do you mean?" Amara asks.

"She got picked up for solicitation the other day. Pretty much been strung out since before the trial. Look how thin she's gotten...you can see her track marks from here," he says, pointing inconspicuously.

"Can you blame her?" Amara replies.

"Suppose I can't," he says, arching his eyebrows. "They cut her a deal. She'll have to go to rehab to stay out of jail, though." Amara nods as Carter leans back in his chair and begins looking through his phone.

"I'm surprised more members of the jury didn't show," James Edwards says. He casts a bored glance around the room. He was the jury's foreman. He's sitting with his arms folded, taking stock of the others as he pushes his glasses up. James is sitting next to another juror, Cynthia Hallsley. She's tan with long black hair. She wears a dark brown dress and appears apprehensive as she sits with her legs crossed.

"Maybe they're too squeamish," Cynthia replies, shifting in her seat.

"Maybe so. But I had to see it for myself. It's so awful, what he did," James says, shaking his head.

Cynthia draws a nervous breath through her nose and nods.

The warden walks in, wearing a dark gray suit and black tie. He's in his early fifties with dark brown hair that's slicked back. "All right, everyone, looks like we're about ready to get started. I just want to remind y'all that this is a two-way mirror," he says, stepping toward the glass and pointing at it. "He cannot see you. He cannot hear you. He will have the opportunity to speak his last words, so if anyone wants to leave now or before that happens, that'll be fine." He pauses before asking, "Does anyone have any last-minute questions?"

Everyone stares at him in silence. "All right then, it should be just a few more minutes," he says in a quiet, comforting tone. He takes his seat on the first row on the opposite end from Mollie. The man seems anxious as he wipes his brow and sits upright in his chair.

The room falls silent when the door on the other side of the window opens. I walk inside, escorted by two guards. I am wearing hand and feet shackles. They jangle against my orange jumpsuit as I amble along. They've forced me to wear the mask again. My head is to the ground and my hair is greasy and matted; it covers most of my face.

The guards trod me along until I reach a medical chair in the center of the room. They have me sit down on it. Then they remove my hand and wrist shackles, keeping their grip tight on my arms. Each lowers me onto the chair and fastens me down, using its thick leather straps; my chest, arms, and legs are bound tightly.

The lights are quite overpowering inside. I squint across the room, trying to see through the window. I cannot. I know they are watching me. I only wish I could see their faces—but instead, the cowards hide behind their little glass pane.

A doctor and a nurse step inside. The nurse is wheeling a little medical cart with a device attached to it. It has three plungers on it with different colored solutions inside. I can taste it already, the intravenous liquor of my ruin. The nurse wipes my arm clean with a sterile pad. Then she sticks a needle that's connected to the machine inside my vein and tapes it down.

A strange feeling of calm comes over me. My chest rises and falls without effort. I know what awaits, and I do not care what happens next. "Mr. Asher...." the doctor begins, interrupting the passive vacancy within my mind. He tilts his head to meet my gaze. I turn toward him. He's older, maybe around sixty-five, and slightly overweight with barely any hair on the sides of his head.

"You will receive an injection—a lethal cocktail consisting of three parts: Pentobarbital, which is a fast-moving anesthetic to render you unconscious and prevent seizures; Pancuronium bromide, which will paralyze voluntary muscle movement throughout your body, including the lungs and diaphragm; and finally, you'll receive a high dose of potassium chloride, which will stop your heart."

"The barbiturate will put you into a deep state of unconsciousness so that pain will not be felt. Your eyelids will become heavy and close involuntarily. The neurons in your brain will stop firing, your blood vessels will dilate, and your heart muscles will weaken until the cardiovascular system begins to fail. All of this will be followed by a flush of saline solution to speed the flow of drugs throughout your body. You will be asleep during the procedure and completely unaware of what is happening. Do you have any questions before we begin?"

I feel slightly perturbed that this impotent old man has intruded upon my peaceful isolation. I grunt in reply, and he stares at me patiently for several seconds, waiting to see if I'll say anything else.

"Very well, Mr. Asher. Do you have any last words before we start this process?"

Last words. I should have thought of this. It's in all the movies, after all. Several seconds pass in silence, and just when the doctor begins to speak, I interrupt him. "Yes. I do have some thoughts to share."

I clear my throat. My eyes shift toward the floor and then to the window. I stare through it, hoping to pierce the glass with my cold, empty eyes. The room is entirely silent, save for the howling wind outside. It shakes the trees and a large branch scratches against the window. I stare at them for several seconds longer as the howling and grating continue.

"This is not my end," I begin in a low, brooding tone. "I will not be stricken down. The Dark Lord has empowered me anew, and all trespassers will be bound in blood. Your shallow, empty process, it may claim my life, but there is no power beyond that. Take my body, but this soul, its purpose...they will endure, and I shall have my revenge."

Both rooms fall silent once I stop speaking. The wind howls loudly as I glare at my spectators through the glass. It's starting to rain heavily again, and the pounding drops slap hard against the outside window. Only my eyes are visible behind the mask, and they are wreathed in vile hatred. My disdain pierces the window while I pour blackness into each and every one of their souls. *You will be mine*, my eyes say to theirs.

On the other side of the glass, the onlookers remain silent; each of them leans over in their seat while they return my gaze with worry and confusion.

The doctor allows this to persist for nearly half a minute longer as he watches me with fascination. He's growing quite uncomfortable; I can see it in my periphery, but I pay him no mind. I breathe heavily and my hands are balled into fists. "We will now begin the procedure," he mutters, intruding upon my spiteful solace once again.

The doctor begins busying himself with something on the machine. He presses several buttons, and the system beeps twice in response. It makes a loud whirring sound as it begins powering on. Little pumps begin moving up and down inside the machine. There's a loud cracking sound from outside that pierces the white noise. It sounds like a tree being violently ripped apart. The lights flicker for a second, but we are not in darkness for long, because the emergency power kicks on.

The lights are dimmer now. "Did we just lose power?" the nurse questions.

The doctor casts a worried glance to the nearby window, observing the torrential downpour outside. "I think so...but we'll be all right. The emergency power will hold. We should be fine to proceed," he says.

She nods and then checks my restraints one last time. After seeing that they are still tight, the nurse looks back at the doctor. He draws a deep breath before pressing a series of buttons on the machine. It beeps once in a low, flat tone. The first plunger drops, and it pumps a dense, green liquid into my veins. The machine beeps twice in a higher pitch, and then the second plunger drops. It beeps twice more, and the third plunger fills me with purple fluid through the IV.

I start to feel drowsy once I feel the poison entering my body. My eyelids are growing heavier with each passing second. It seems I am all set to fall into endless slumber when I feel a sudden, sharp pain coursing throughout my body. "Aggghhhh!" I scream. The doctor looks away from the machine and then stares at me in alarm. He stands from his seat and looks between the machine and me quickly, trying to figure out what has gone wrong.

I struggle against my straps while the veins in my arms and forehead bulge. I throw my head back and forth against the hospital bed. Knives and daggers swim through me, and I am in pure, unrefined agony.

In the other room, Cynthia is clutching onto a crucifix that hangs from her neck. She's leaning on the edge of her seat, staring with her mouth agape. Horrified, she reaches out and grabs James' hand. He's entranced by the grotesque scene unfolding before him. They clasp one another's hands tightly as the seconds drag on.

"What's he doing?!" the nurse exclaims.

"I—I don't know," the doctor says, shaking his head. He is standing between the equipment and me, examining everything in a feverish rush. His head darts back and forth as he tries to figure out what to do next.

"Agghhh!" I continue screeching. "Stop! Make it stop...you god-damned," my voice grows quieter as my eyes begin to twitch.

The blood pumping through my body comes to an abrupt standstill. My struggle subsides. The pained, baleful light leaves my eyes, making them empty and glazed. The monitor next to me flatlines, and suddenly, I am dead.

VI.

Atlanta Department of Corrections

January 21, 2025

12:15 a.m.

The doctor rushes over and checks my pulse. "He's gone." He looks over at the nurse with his jaw hanging open. The man seems relieved, as if he were the one who had suffered the terrible ordeal. The nurse stares back at him with dismay.

"Mark the time," the doctor orders as he comes back to his senses.

"It's 12:15," the nurse reports promptly. She annotates the time in a brown ledger.

The doctor doesn't look at her. He takes a seat next to me and stares at my inert corpse with some sense of resignation. "Write it in the log," he replies. She nods. It seems all the excitement has taken everything out of the old man, and he can't help but wonder why things didn't go as planned.

On the other side of the window, no one has moved a muscle. The room is frozen in time as each of them sits rigidly in their chair. After a moment's silence, the warden stands slowly from his seat. He turns and faces the rest of them; he's unsure of what to say.

"What the hell just happened in there?" Jeff questions him. His voice is pushy and perturbed; he stares at the warden expectantly with his notepad in hand.

"I...uh," the warden begins uncertainly. His forehead gleams with sweat. He's still staring through the window as he begins addressing them. "We'll be launching a full investigation into this evening's events, so I'll have to get back to you on that." He looks around the room, not really meeting anyone's gaze. You can tell he'd rather be anywhere else on Earth at the moment. "Thank you all for coming. I'm afraid I won't be taking any more questions at this time."

Jeff seems agitated by the warden's nonresponsive answer. He arches his eyebrows, shakes his head, and then looks to the ground with disgust. Everyone starts gathering their belongings and standing from their seats. They each make their way out of the room in a strained, mournful silence.

Chapter Five

I.

Eastview Cemetery

January 23, 2025

10:00 a.m.

Amara and Carter make their way down a narrow, paved trail that runs through a lightly populated cemetery. Pink, yellow, and purple flowers adorn the graves of those who've passed. The sky above is heavy with dark clouds as thin sunlight attempts to peek through.

Carter is wearing a black suit and a dark blue tie; Amara's forest green dress practically blends in with the drab setting surrounding her. "I can't believe he's finally dead...after all that," she says, her voice coming cold and detached.

"Yeah. Hope he enjoys his time in hell, the miserable bastard," Carter comments.

She chuckles casually to acknowledge him.

"They're all like that, you know? The serials. You'll see it too. Angry. Full of fight. Right up until that last moment...when their eyes roll into their back of their skull," he adds.

"Did they ever get back to you about what went wrong?"

"Yeah. Doctor told me there was a kink in the tubing. Guess the needle was also pointing in the wrong direction. He said it would've stopped some of the chemicals from flowing. Probably put him in a lot of pain too—but it's not like the man didn't deserve it," he replies.

The two detectives stop in front of an empty grave. Two men are standing inside the hole; little tufts of dirt hit the ground as they continue digging. They're both covered in sweat and wearing stained gray coveralls. They rest their shovels for a moment, look up at the detectives, and nod. Carter nods back as they stand over the open hole.

"Guess that's why he freaked out," she says.

"Well, I'm glad he didn't just fall asleep. It should've been a lot worse," he replies. Carter takes a pack of cigarettes from his coat pocket and lights one as they stand over the grave. Amara looks at Carter with disappointment. "It's my last one, I swear," he says, smiling apologetically.

She smirks and shakes her head. "Yeah, I've heard that one before."

"Doc says I have to now," Carter replies. He takes another drag and then ashes on the ground as they continue watching the men work below.

"Oh, Jesus Christ!" one of them yells. The detectives lean over and see a swirling pit of black snakes; they're fighting against themselves in an angry, tangled web. The two men scramble to get out of the hole. "Good God almighty!" he goes on. He's about forty with a scraggly beard and bright red hair. He takes his cap off and wipes the sweat from his brow as he stares back into the hole from whence he came. "I've seen a lot of shit out here, but goddamn...that just about gave me a heart attack."

"You and me both," the other says, guffawing nervously. He's younger than the other one, baby-faced with short light brown hair. "That'll have to be deep enough," he says, shaking his head.

The other nods in agreement. He turns to Carter and shrugs. Then the two men head down the narrow path toward the little guard house by the cemetery entrance.

"Strange…" Carter observes.

"What?" Amara asks.

"They don't usually burrow down that far," he says, taking a long drag of his cigarette and staring into the pit. The snakes continue fighting against one another for a moment and then gradually make their way out of the hole. They take off in separate directions once they reach the ground; the detectives step back cautiously and watch them slither away. "Mmm…I hate snakes," he says, grimacing.

Carter turns his head and spots a priest coming down the walkway toward them. He's in his mid-fifties, thin with fading blonde hair, and dressed in all black except for the white of his collar. "You'd think they wouldn't even bother," Carter says, smirking. He flicks his cigarette butt, and it sails into the nearby grass.

"Good morning, Detectives," the priest greets them as he approaches.

"Good morning, Father," Carter replies.

"I'm Father Bishop," he tells them. "They said to expect you." The man smiles before shaking each of their hands. "I don't suppose you know if anyone else is coming?"

Carter chuckles while he exhales smoke. "I doubt it."

"No family?"

Carter glances at Amara. "We couldn't find any. Hell, I doubt even the man's mother would want to claim him, assuming she's still alive."

Father Bishop chuckles nervously and then glances around the cemetery with his hands in his pockets. "Well, I guess we should go ahead and get started, then," he mutters.

"Suppose so," Carter replies. "Let me just give 'em a call, tell them we're ready for the body." He steps away and pulls out his cell phone. Carter dials a number and then begins speaking quietly into the phone.

Father Bishop smiles and nods to Amara. "Can I ask you something, Father?" she says, putting her hands in her jacket pockets and staring into the distance.

"Of course."

"How do you do it?" she replies, shifting her gaze back to him. He looks at her with some confusion, waiting for her to continue. "How do you ask for forgiveness, for blessing...for a man like that?" she says, nodding toward the gravestone.

"All of God's children deserve love," he begins slowly. "I can't say that I'll ever understand what this man did, but God can always see what we're unable to." She nods as he continues, "No one is beyond salvation...no matter how awful they may be on Earth," he says, looking at the gravestone with disappointment.

Amara reflects on his words for a moment before replying, "Can't say it's something I could do."

Father Bishop smiles at her politely. Carter ends his call and then walks back toward them. "They said they'd be down in just a few," he reports.

Several minutes pass as Carter and Father Bishop make small talk. Amara is crossing her arms and examining the surrounding graves from afar. From the distance, she spots four men carrying a pine casket. As they grow closer, she can see that it's quite plain, no ornate markings, no special engravements.

The four men approach the vacant gravestone and set the casket down near the open hole. One of them jumps inside and grabs the two shovels that were left behind. The others set up a pulley system with metal posts placed along each corner. The men pick the casket back up and set it down over the grave. They use the pulley straps to gently lower the box into the earth. As the others retrieve their ropes and supports, one of them motions for Carter's attention.

"Here's to it, Father," Carter says, nodding toward the grave.

Father Bishop turns and then begins walking slowly toward the headstone. He looks to the sky and observes the darkening clouds. They've grown heavy and dense with various shades of gray and black. He stops before the open hole and stares at the stone in front of it. Only the name and the dates are inscribed on it; nothing else is worthy of remembrance.

The detectives follow behind Father Bishop, flanking him on either side. The middle-aged priest pulls a Bible out of a small satchel that he'd carried with him. He holds the book close; his eyes dart around nervously, and it seems he's unsure of where to begin. "Lord...it is not every day that we are tasked with such a high charge of forgiveness. Most of your flock will never stray as far from your light as the soul of Dalton Asher." Father Bishop pauses, struggling to find the right words.

"But we know, Lord, that no soul is beyond redemption. For you tell us in Isaiah 55 to 'let the wicked one abandon his way and the sinful one his thoughts; let him return to the Lord, so that he may have compassion on him, and to our God, for he will freely forgive...' Lord, we ask that you forgive this angry, misguided soul. We ask, Father, that you show mercy on him as he is laid to rest. And we ask that the harm he's brought into this world be undone, and that you show compassion on him from above."

Father Bishop stops there, giving his shaky voice a rest. He draws a deep breath through his nose, purging himself of all negative feelings. "Amen," he says at last, nodding his head with gentle resolution. He turns slowly and faces the others.

"Think you could have saved the kind words, Padre," Carter says scornfully. "This one...he doesn't deserve your mercy." He clears his throat, leans forward, and then spits on the gravestone. Carter glares at it with disgust. "Sometimes a man's just beyond salvation," he says, putting his hands in his coat pockets.

Father Bishop looks at Carter with mild disappointment and then nods his head. The two detectives start heading down the path as Father Bishop glances back at the headstone one last time. He catches up to them, and they walk together in silence toward the cemetery gate.

II.

Eastview Cemetery

January 24, 2025

12:15 a.m.

The night is cold and dark as the groundskeeper makes his final round for the evening. He shines his flashlight across the cemetery grounds while he ambles along. He's about forty, wearing a dark red flannel shirt with blue jeans and work boots. He puts his free hand in his pocket to keep it from the cold wind that blows.

The man walks with his head down, scanning the grounds with his flashlight. But he stops when he sees the lot's newest addition. He settles his light upon the stone. "Dalton Lee Asher, November 15, 1989 - January 21, 2025," it reads. He stares at it and shudders; a disconcerting chill runs up his spine and forces him to move along.

The man returns to the guard shack, fumbles with his keys for a moment, and then opens the door. He yawns as he walks inside and shuts the door behind him. Tiredly, he crawls into a small twin bed in the corner where he plans on retiring for the evening.

Outside, the cold, calm breeze continues. The sparse leaves that remain on the trees sway gently under its force. Along the path, there's a trash can, and two stray dogs rifle through it hungrily. A radiant, full moon hangs above; its amber and gold light shines through the gray clouds that drift by aimlessly.

The two dogs tear open a paper bag of rotting fast food and begin fighting over its half-eaten contents. They knock over the trashcan, and it spills out onto the walkway. Bits of paper and debris begin tumbling across the pavement and scatter along the grass. An empty cup drifts past a row of headstones.

A large, black serpent slithers his way among the graves. He stops along a patch of freshly disturbed earth and then creeps up the stone in front of it. His thick, scaly body slinks its way up the rock. He's about six feet long, thick, with beady, hateful eyes. The head bobs gently, taking in its surroundings as the forked tongue tastes the barren night air.

A dirty pale hand emerges from the earth. The fingers grasp and fumble as it pushes through the soil. The snake fixates on the new movement. The arm extends further out as the hand reaches toward the sky. The arm begins moving back and forth, creating a wider hole in the ground. The top of a head crowns through the dirt, then struggles against it, freeing itself from submersion.

The head wriggles free while the mouth spits clumps of soil and grass. Spiders crawl from the opening that it creates. The hair is long, black, and matted. A second arm emerges. Now they push down against the soil, pressing the body from its bondage. Its lips widen and the tongue flails as it bellows into the night. After a moment's effort, the torso is above ground. The arms extend as the hands claw and scratch at the earth. This wretched, pale being exerts itself to no end as it rises free from damnation.

The corpse drags its legs and feet from the earth below. The body is on all fours now—it's wild and breathing heavily. Saliva drips from the crusted lips, and snot pours from its nostrils with every chalky breath. Angry, bloodshot eyes stare hard into the ground.

And at this moment, I begin to wonder, am I me? Could this be real? My veins pulse as I clench the dirt with both hands. I raise a fistful of soil in front of me and watch it sift through my fingers. *It's real enough.*

I grunt loudly as I stagger to my feet. My body feels like it weighs a thousand pounds, though I'm quite emaciated. My eyes scour the cemetery grounds, and I see a small flock of black birds take flight from their branches.

I'm still gasping for air. It's like something catches inside my chest with every painful breath I take. I stretch my hands out in front of me and examine them. I'm paler than before, bloodless, and cold.

I focus my bleary eyes on the plain stone before me. It's my name written upon it. That's undeniable. I hear a crow caw behind me, and I turn to see it. I can't find the bird but instead notice that a collection of trash is rustling down the path and into the grass; something about its freedom entrances me.

A loud, intrusive noise forces me to turn back around. It's a horn honking and the sound of tires peeling against asphalt. I look beyond the cemetery gate and watch the car drive down the street. Its headlights nearly blind me as it approaches. I cover my eyes to shield them from the offensive light. The car passes by, but it has revealed to me what was not known before.

Because suddenly, I see him staring at me, as if he were lying in wait this entire time. My jaw drops and my eyes widen as I take a single step toward the watching serpent. I fall to my knees in awe. I am humbled by his sheer magnificence.

The majestic snake rises from his coil, and his presence is overwhelming. I can feel his power pressing my body down; I couldn't stand if I wanted to. He continues staring back at me. His eyes are illuminating; they penetrate me to my core. Suddenly, I know everything that I've ever wanted to know.

I am empowered beyond my wildest dreams, but still, I am held frozen in place, awaiting his command.

The sky and the scene around me grow black in an instant. No light peers through the blanketing abyss. The serpent and I are left alone in the void. We are racing through the cosmos together as I kneel before him. He is projecting something inside of me, and I welcome it with every fiber of my being. He feeds me in ways that I cannot describe; I have never felt so full, so satiated in all my life.

My tattered clothes catch fire. I stare down at my hands and arms as the black suit is devoured by hungry flames. It does not scorch my skin; I feel only pleasure—pure physical bliss unlike any other I have ever known. It steals my breath away, and I feel orgasmic as the flames scorch every thread of clothing from my body.

I am entirely naked when I hear his dreadful call. It is more than a voice, more than simple sound waves ringing within my ears. It is the rhythm of music. "*My child,*" he calls to me. The voice comes not from the snake, but from the empty black surrounding him. I begin to weep. Tears of pure joy stream down my cheeks as I lose myself inside the serpent's powerful voice. "I have waited for you," he tells me in a calm, deep whisper.

"Are you really here with me...now, after all this time?" I ask. My voice trembles as a chill passes through me.

"I am everywhere," he whispers. "And I have never stopped watching."

"What must I do?" My voice breaks as I beg for the answer.

"You know your task," he responds a low, menacing tone. "Come to me," he beckons.

My legs shake as I begin standing upright. I am shocked to see that my feet are still planted in the earth. As I look down upon them, the black landscape has vanished, and we are back in the cemetery where we began. In this moment, I have completed my journey, returning home the victor after war and tribulation.

I'm standing over the mighty serpent now, and he looks up at me, perched atop the gravestone. "Give me your hand," he commands. I look down at him with some confusion. Then I cup my hands together and lower them to my waist. They quake as I offer them to the serpent.

The snake moves forward and then begins crawling up my arm. His long, powerful body feels heavy as he slinks his way up. The end of his tail is still on the grave as his head pushes past my chest. Then he draws himself back while I gaze upon him.

Our eyes meet. His little black pools grow into vast, endless oceans. They strip my mind of all thoughts as I stare into them. My pupils disappear entirely; I am lost within his power. I breathe heavily while my lips quiver, and I grow cold within.

I can feel my mouth opening and my jaw dropping, though I do not command them to do so. It is stretching my face to impossible lengths as my jaw hangs lower and lower. It feels as though the edges of my lips will tear and my jaw will dislocate by the time it finally stops.

A shapeless black mass forms behind me. My eyes and jaw are frozen in place. The snake sticks his head inside of my mouth. I stand there, gagging, but I cannot move. My body is rigid. I can feel his thick body stretching my throat and esophagus. It's deeply painful. A large lump forms on my neck as he continues slithering his way down.

After a few seconds, the snake finishes working his way inside. I have consumed him entirely. The lump on my neck vanishes while he pushes his way deeper within. I fall to the ground, and a fit of retching overtakes me. I feel sick but cannot vomit. The black mass encircles me like a dense, heavy mist. It tastes like bitter tar upon my tongue. Smoke fills my lungs as my vision becomes hazy.

The nausea passes after a moment. Something inside of me clicks into place. My eyes glow a pale blue as I make my way back to my feet. His deep, terrible voice begins flowing through me. "Slaughter those who've stolen from us, humiliated us...feel my power reign within you—and rape the meek." I hold my arms in front of me; every vein inside of them pulses with his dominance.

He is I, and we are one. My eyes glow brightly as I stare into the city scene beyond the outer gate. I can taste their flesh; I can hear their screams. My teeth have grown sharp as razors while the hunger surges inside me. I am strong, more capable than ever before. The breeze blows my long dark hair back as I stand wide in the cemetery, naked and proud.

Chapter Six

I.

Fulton County District Attorney's Office

January 24, 2025

6:30 p.m.

Henry Adams strolls down a white tiled hallway toward his office. The man is visibly excited. He beams with confidence with his head held high. Henry is wearing a baby blue designer suit with a bright red tie. He passes by a row of bulletin boards posted along the walls and stops at the door with his name displayed on it.

Henry leaves one hand in his pocket as he opens the door to his office. He strides in blithely. "Ha-ha!" he exclaims, punching the air confidently. Henry removes his jacket and hangs it on a coat rack near the door. "God-damn right," the zealot continues while he loosens his tie. He takes it off and drapes it over a chair in front of his desk.

Henry walks behind the desk, rolls out his large leather chair, and takes a seat. He props his feet up on the desk and breathes deeply through his nostrils. Then he places his hands on his head and leans back for a moment, basking. The man smiles to himself, relishing in some apparent victory. He studies the walls of his office, taking it all in: his degrees from prominent universities, rows of crimson law books, and several awards and placards detailing his accomplishments.

After about half a minute, something dawns on him. Henry takes his feet down. He smirks as he picks up his office phone and starts dialing quickly. He runs his fingers through his hair as he waits for an answer.

"Hello," a female voice greets him on the other end.

He giggles a little to himself and says, "Guess who got it?"

"You didn't..." she gushes. "You got the conviction?"

"Told you to have a little faith," he says, grinning as he leans back in his chair.

"Wow...You're really coming up. First the Asher case, and now this one? People are going to notice. Won't be long before your name is on a campaign ticket somewhere."

He places his hand on the large oak desk and spreads his fingers out, drumming them against the wood. "Katherine...you're making me blush. What do you say we get together, have a little drink to celebrate?"

There's a long pause on the other end of the line. A few seconds pass. Then Katherine sighs and says, "I don't know, Hank. I'm pretty swamped. You know, yours wasn't the only big case on the docket."

Henry frowns. "Aw, come on, there's always tomorrow. Besides, I could come over to help you...*catch up.*"

She chuckles at his remark. "Yeah, like all the 'catching up' we did last time?" she asks.

"What can I say? I can't help myself around you," he says, leaning over the desk, and lowering his voice.

She laughs again. "I'm sure you tell that to all your little girlfriends..." Katherine sighs and waits a few seconds, keeping him held in suspense. "All right, *one* drink. And you're not staying over. I've got an early morning with the DA tomorrow."

"Our usual spot, then?" he asks, his voice coming low and sly.

She thinks for a moment and replies, "Yeah, I can meet you in, uh, let's say an hour?"

"I'll see you there, gorgeous." Henry smiles to himself as they hang up. He bites his lip and nods his head as he stands up from the desk. Then he walks toward the coat rack, grabs his suit jacket, and puts it on. Henry checks himself in a mirror that's hanging by the door. He straightens his collar while studying his reflection.

Henry opens the office door and begins walking down the hallway with a spring in his step. He turns left and exits through the courthouse doors. Then he walks down the wide concrete steps, running his hand along the rail as he descends. He has not a care in the world as he reaches the bottom.

Henry walks toward the parking lot on his right. The sun has nearly gone now; the sky is filled with red, orange, and purple hues as twilight approaches. He pulls his keys out of his pocket and unlocks a newer black BMW as he walks toward it.

I peek my head above the bushes while I crouch low, watching him from a spot near the courthouse entrance. My eyes have lost their bluish glow, and my teeth have returned to normal. Their razor's edge is gone, but my Dark Lord has assured me that they'll return...if ever I need them.

My skin remains unnaturally pale, and my lips are a faded, translucent pink. I've managed to find some new garb—or rather I've managed to take it violently from another creature of the night. I wear a long dark coat, black pants, and combat boots. A pair of sunglasses shield my eyes from the fading sun.

Henry is about twenty yards away now. He can't hear the rustling of the bushes while I emerge from hiding. I step out onto the sidewalk and watch him get inside of his car. I clench my fist, staring at him from the walkway as he takes his seat. I scrape my long, dirty nails against the palm of my left hand while I watch him drive away, and in my right, a long bowie knife with a black handle hangs down by my side. A subtle grin spreads across my lips as I start walking down the path.

II.

Outside of the Tennessee Tavern

January 24, 2025

11:45 p.m.

Henry steps outside of the Tennessee Tavern in good spirits. He has his arm around Katherine's waist. She's about thirty-five and has fiery red hair. Katherine is very thin with a fair complexion. She's wearing a black dress and her matching heels clack loudly against the pavement while they walk together. Henry's collar is unbuttoned, and he carries his jacket with two fingers as it's slung across his back. They're still laughing together when they enter the parking lot.

They stop once they reach a silver Mercedes. Katherine leans against the driver's side door as Henry takes her in his arms. He runs his hands along her body as they kiss. They settle at her waist while he draws her in closer. She pulls her head back and smiles mischievously. "*Not* tonight, I said."

"Aw, pretty please," he begs, leaning in as he kisses her neck. "You can't spare a few minutes?"

She laughs. "A few minutes, huh?"

He breathes heavily against her skin and sighs. "You know what I mean," he whispers.

"No...not tonight," she says, leaning away from him. "I really do have to be in early."

He looks at her with pouty lips.

"Oh, I don't think that's going to do it, mister," she says, flashing her teeth while she shakes her head. "Besides, aren't I supposed to be *your* boss?"

"You can boss me around any way you'd like," he says, leaning in to kiss her again.

Katherine throws her head back playfully, reveling in her ability to tease him. Henry kisses her neck for a few seconds longer, then she raises two fingers to his chin and forces him to make eye contact. "You know, mama always told me if a man is any good, he'll wait for it." She smiles and kisses him once on the lips. Katherine unlocks her Mercedes and opens the door. She interlaces their fingers, then outstretches her arm. Henry tilts his head, kissing her hand.

"You're breakin' my heart," he tells her.

"Guess you can't win 'em all," she says, grinning as she takes her black leather seat.

Henry leans against the opened door and looks down at her, smiling. "We'll see about that…"

She starts the car and raises her eyebrows. "See you round the office, handsome."

Henry chuckles and then shuts the door. He grins at Katherine through the window and watches her while she drives away. Henry grunts to himself and then takes his car keys from his pocket as he begins walking across the lot toward his BMW.

He unlocks the car and hops inside. Henry reaches down and grabs an electronic cigarette in the cup holder. He starts vaping as he leans back in his seat. "Whole lot of effort…" he complains while shaking his head. He takes his cell phone from his pocket and then begins scrolling through his contacts. "But the night's not over yet," Henry goes on.

"Ah, Jessica…" he croons. Henry smirks to himself as he begins texting. He waits for her reply while he scans the parking lot out of boredom.

He yawns faintly as his phone dings with a new message. Henry smiles as he reads it and begins nodding his head. He cranks the ignition and then punches an address into his car's GPS. Then he turns the radio up and starts driving away. "Who says you can't win 'em all?" Henry mutters, grinning widely as he pulls the car out of the lot.

A few minutes pass as Henry makes his way through the darkened city. Duran Duran's "Hungry Like the Wolf" is playing on the radio, and he begins singing along with the chorus. He's gripping the steering wheel and belting out the lyrics while he makes his way toward his destination.

I can't take much more of this asshole's self-congratulation, his smug overconfidence. I am lying on the floorboards of his backseat. A silver handgun rests atop my chest. I clench it with both hands and breathe as little as possible.

Henry turns the radio up even louder. I begin to make my move. I shift the pistol to my left hand and raise my right arm on the seat. Then I start hoisting myself up slowly as I study his face in the rearview mirror.

We're stopped at a traffic light just before the entrance of a long tunnel. The streets around us are practically deserted. Henry continues singing with his eyes closed. I wait for the light to change before I continue moving. After a moment, the whimsical man reopens his eyes, and we start driving forward again.

The dim orange lights of the tunnel surround us now as we begin moving through them. The song ends, and Henry's phone dings with a new message. It's placed on a hands-free mount on his dash; he stares at it for several seconds while he reads.

I finally finish raising myself onto the seat behind him. I'm sitting upright now, glaring at Henry through the rearview mirror. A single second passes before he notices my movement. His eyes widen with alarm as he turns his head toward me.

"Hi," I greet him cordially. My teeth glisten in the dark as my smile spreads. Henry begins shouting obscenities while his confusion grows. I wait for him to settle down.

"Who the fuck are you?!" Henry screams. Panicked, he reaches inside the glovebox and begins rifling around anxiously. He sifts through the papers and junk inside. His nervous eyes flit between the unfurling road and the stranger sitting behind him.

"Looking for this?" I question calmly. My smile has faded now, and I'm serious as a heart attack. I hold the pistol in my right hand. It dangles from my fingers as I hold it by the trigger guard. I glance at the gun as if it's some strange, foreign object. I can't help but grin at Henry's dismay.

"Jesus fucking Christ," he mutters to himself. He begins realizing his situation and then slumps back into his seat. "What, uh, what do you want?" he asks in a quick, flat tone. A strange air of acceptance has fallen around him like little flakes of ashes.

"I want you to look at me," I order him. He glances up at me through the rearview mirror, and our eyes meet for a split second. "No, really look at me," I command.

He sighs and turns his head toward me. "What do you want?" he repeats. "I'll give you everything I have," he says, giving me his most serious, pleading eyes. Henry glances between me and the road but continues looking at me as instructed.

"You don't recognize me, do you?" I ask. He squints at me in the low light, straining his eyes to see.

"Come on, Hank, haven't you missed me?" Henry stares for a few seconds longer, and then suddenly, something clicks inside his brain.

Henry's expression slowly changes from dread to anger. I start bellowing with deep, rich laughter. As he opens his lips to speak, I thump him hard on the head with the pistol's muzzle. He swerves after I strike him, but he manages to get back into his lane quickly. The muzzle leaves a stinging, red imprint on his forehead. He reels back in his seat and grimaces, touching his fingertips to the point of impact. I continue laughing as he groans and curses under his breath.

After a few seconds, my laughter dies down. Henry stops complaining but continues rubbing his throbbing head. His breath is ragged, and his pulse has quickened, I can feel it. He's a volatile mix of contained rage and stoked fear. "I don't know how you're doing this, or what you hope to achieve, but I'll kill us both...I swear, I'll do it."

I place a friendly hand on his back and smile. "As fun as that sounds, Hank, I doubt it." I pat him on the shoulder as he ponders my words. I draw my hand back and lean against the leather seat. Then I throw my head back and sprawl out luxuriously. "But I don't want to live forever, do you?" My voice comes as an unhurried melancholy.

Several seconds of silence pass between us. "What can I give you?" he asks. "There must be *something* you want. I, I could get your conviction overturned...I could set this all straight. Everything could go back to the way it was."

I raise the pistol to my mouth and start chewing on the end of it lightly as I ponder his offer. "What do I want? What do *I* want?" I say, stretching out the syllables while I repeat myself. "I want you to *die*, weapon of God!"

I set the pistol down and take hold of his neck from behind. I start squeezing tightly. His eyes bulge, and the car swerves as he begins losing focus. I erupt into wild, inhuman laughter; it is the dry sound of a cackling hyena. I can feel the Dark Lord working through me; his presence floods my veins as my heart beats faster.

Henry's head starts sagging, but he continues fighting against me. He tries prying my fingers from his throat. When he can't manage to do so, Henry turns his head far to the right and bites me hard on the knuckles.

Then he begins losing control of the car. We scrape against the wall inside the tunnel. It makes a terrible sound as the metal grates against concrete. Henry overcorrects, and we collide into the side of a passing car in the neighboring lane. The other car slows and then pulls over, but Henry continues driving. He starts accelerating. The man is trying to frighten me, but it won't work. I continue squeezing, despite the bleeding bitemarks that he's left on my hand.

We've exited the tunnel now, and we're coming fast down a long, sloped street. I gaze down at the speedometer. We're going about fifty miles an hour as we cruise through a residential area. It's filled with high rise apartments and dimly lit corner stores.

Henry keeps pushing his chin down so that I can't restrict his airway. But my efforts are working; I can see him growing weaker as I stare at him through the rearview mirror. I lean in close, bringing my head next to his. I'm squeezing with all my might as his face becomes flush. It continues turning redder and redder, and just when I think I have him, we crash into a parked car.

III.

Downtown Atlanta

January 25, 2025

12:10 a.m.

The hood of Henry's BMW is crushed as it strikes the rear end of a red Toyota sedan. Metal crunches into metal as the two vehicles become one. I am launched through the windshield, and my body sails over the top of the red car. I land on top of its hood. Bits of broken glass are stuck deeply within my skin. A breathless moan escapes my lips as I roll onto my side.

But now I've rolled too far, and my body slides onto the pavement with a heavy thud. My lungs feel as if they're failing me as I begin to crawl. I lurch forward slowly, dragging my knees and elbows against the pavement. Blood drips from my forehead and starts obscuring my vision. I raise a hand up to my eyes and wipe them as I struggle to breathe.

I pause for a moment and collect myself. I catch my breath and strengthen my resolve. Then I place my palms on the pavement and start hoisting myself up—it is an act of sheer will. I finish raising myself and come to a kneeling position. My head bobs as I linger there, dazed. My hair is clumped and matted. I raise my hand to my forehead and feel a small pool of blood near my right temple. Then I lower the hand and stare down at the gore.

"Hey! Hey, man, are you all right?!" a concerned citizen cries. The man's around sixty with feathery white hair. He's wearing a tucked in polo shirt, tan jacket, and blue jeans. He rushes to me from the sidewalk, raising a hand to his glasses to keep them on his face. "Oh my God..." the man goes on as he crouches next to me.

The old man puts a hand on my shoulder and tries to look me in the eyes. I do not meet his gaze. Instead, I continue staring at the pavement as my mind wanders. It's dark out here. There aren't many cars out at this time of night. Only sparse streetlights and a few rays from nearby stores light the area around us.

"Hang on, buddy, I'm going to call for help," the Good Samaritan tells me. Then he reaches into his coat pocket, pulls out a cell phone, and dials 9-1-1.

I draw my boot knife from its sheath as the man looks away; he begins speaking to the operator. As he starts to stand up, I stab him in the gut. His jaw drops as the blade enters his flesh. His eyes widen while he stares at me in shock. I place my free hand on his back to drive the blade in further. He staggers and then falls to his knees. I use him as support to get myself back onto my feet.

As I'm drawing the blade back, I hear something—the opening of a car door. I toss the man's body aside as I rise. I do not bother looking down at him; he is of no consequence. The car door creaks open slowly. A foot emerges, and from about thirty feet away, I can see that the good counselor has survived. Glass crunches beneath his feet as he exits the vehicle. Henry's woozy and unstable. He's leaning against the car door as he gapes at me in awe. Our eyes meet, and he shakes his drowsy little head in disbelief.

Henry turns away from me and starts heading down the street in the opposite direction. He takes a few steps, then stumbles, and falls on his side. Henry grunts and grimaces as he starts forcing himself back up immediately. His movements are jerky and panicked. He can feel the peril that he's in.

I begin lurching toward him. Pain radiates from my knees to my hips as I wobble with every step. But this won't stop me. I push myself through the agony and begin closing the distance between us. He's only about fifteen feet away now. The knife hangs by my side as I continue advancing.

Henry makes it back onto his feet and starts limping away as fast as he can. I'm moving a bit faster, though my left leg is dragging against the pavement like a stiff wooden plank. He shoots a worried glance behind him. Henry can see how close I am now, that he's failing to escape me. His breath quickens, and he lets out a pitiful, aimless whimper. His eyes are desperately darting around the area; his head turns as he scours the streets and buildings surrounding us.

"Help! He's trying to kill me!" Henry screams. No one's close enough to do anything for him. There're a few pedestrians on the sidewalk about a hundred feet away, but that's it. They gawk at the scene unfolding before them. Up ahead, a man tugs at his girlfriend's arm to stop her advance. He pulls out a cell phone and starts placing a call. They take cover in the doorway of a nearby store but continue staring from the distance.

"Somebody, please help!" Henry cries out again, but it's too late. I've got him. I place a hand on his shoulder and put him off balance. He flails his arms, trying to escape my grasp. As he starts stumbling, I throw my weight on him and tackle the man to the ground.

Henry is wheezing, gasping, and giving me everything he's got. He reaches his arms out, trying to crawl away from me. I mount myself on top of his back. Then I lean down, grab a fistful of hair, and hold the blade to his neck. "Stop moving, or I'll cut your throat," I tell him in a calm, dominating tone.

Henry begins sobbing. "Please, someone help..." he begs.

I glance up at the two bystanders watching us from the distance. I smile casually and then look back down at Henry again. I put my head next to his ear and begin to whisper. "They're not going to help you, Hank. It's just you and me here."

"Please...please, stop," he whines. His voice is breaking, and I can't help but appreciate the utter serenity of his debasement. I have defiled this once proud man, and it feels magnificent. I close my eyes and draw a deep, clearing breath through my nose. The air has never tasted so pure, so sublime.

"I'm sorry!" Henry chokes. The tears are drowning out his voice; he sounds nothing like the valiant man who attacked me in court. "I, I can clear your name," he tells me, his voice coming quick and panicked. "Just give me the chance!"

I chuckle dryly at his proposition, the obvious futility of his pleas. Then I lean back and push his face into the asphalt. "I'm sorry, Counselor, but we've moved beyond the courts of men now."

I raise the blade overhead and then stab him in his right shoulder. Henry cries out in pain as I place both hands atop the handle and press it down with all my might. His breath comes short and shallow. He tries moving his left arm around, but he's too weak, too ineffectual.

I take Henry by the hair again and bash his head against the road as hard as I can. I do it again. And again. And again. I keep doing it until I simply become lost in the motion. His head feels lighter and lighter every time I raise it and drive it down onto the pavement. His blood starts soaking my hand, and I can see that it's splattering onto the road next to us.

I raise his lifeless head one last time and stare at it with disgust and resignation. It's all bloody pulp now. His forehead is oozing, mangled tissue; it drips pink and red. The light has left his eyes. They're frozen and bloodshot; his right orb has lapsed from its socket. Henry's jaw hangs limply. Blood seeps from the corners of his lips.

"Behold," I whisper, half-grinning while I release his head. Some transient sense of relief comes over me, and I feel deeply content. I pause on top of him for a moment, relishing in the completion of my task. Then I begin drawing the knife from his shoulder. The blade is wedged in deeply, and it takes some wriggling to break free.

As I rise to my feet, the black mass returns. It forms behind me, casting a large silhouette that's much broader than my figure. The wind is at my back as I begin walking down the street with my arms spread wide. The knife hangs in my left hand, and I feel weightless—as if I may ascend at any moment and attack the heavens above.

And now it comes, the dark serenity I've waited for. I begin laughing aloud as I walk down the street without a care in the world. As I'm passing by Henry's BMW, I can hear that it's still running. It's quite odd considering the extensive damage to his hood and bumper. Nonetheless, I take it as a good omen. I hop inside and take stock of the vehicle's interior.

Then I put the car into gear. It makes a loud scraping sound as I begin reversing. The headlights are completely extinguished, and there's only faint traces of the windshield remaining. I put the car into drive, and the transmission thuds loudly. A faint clicking runs throughout the car as I drive into the night.

IV.

Downtown Atlanta

January 25, 2025

1:50 a.m.

Amara and Carter ride through the darkened city in silence. Only the sound of the ticking turn signal fills their Crown Victoria as Carter drives along; he stares straight ahead with tired, bleary eyes. He's wearing a black suit with a tan overcoat. Amara gazes out the window and holds a cup of coffee in her lap. She's wearing a dark blue blazer and white blouse underneath.

Carter grunts as he makes a left-hand turn. "Another day, another body," he gripes. As he completes the turn, they see the flashing red and blue lights up ahead. Two marked police cars are blocking a large swath of road toward the bottom of a hill. Four uniformed officers are setting up a wide cordon. A few curious onlookers gather behind the yellow police tape.

Carter pulls up to the scene and then parks along the sidewalk. They get out and start walking toward the yellow tape. A young officer greets them as they approach. "Detectives…" he murmurs, nodding with his hands on his belt.

Carter nods back before crossing under the tape. "What do we got?" he replies, raising his eyebrows, and staring at the man expectantly.

"We responded to a call about thirty minutes ago," the officer reports. He tilts his head while stepping toward the body. Amara and Carter follow behind him. "Couple of witnesses saw the assailant. Looks like the primary victim was a white male, mid-thirties."

"You pull his ID yet?" Amara asks.

The uniform smirks. "Thought I'd leave that to you."

They come to a stop when they reach the body. Carter squats down to get a better look. "Aw, shit. It can't be..." he says, staring with his mouth open. He gazes up at Amara, and she's equally surprised. "I think it is..." she admits reluctantly.

Carter reaches inside the dead man's back pocket and pulls out his wallet. He checks the ID. "Well, I'll be damned...*Henry James Adams*. How the hell did he end up out here?" he asks, glancing around the scene before his eyes settle back onto the corpse sprawled on the pavement. Henry's dead eyes stare back at him; his pulpy flesh is caked in coagulated blood. "And that's the other one over there?" Carter asks, looking up at the uniform.

"Sure is."

"You said there were witnesses?" Amara asks.

"Mm-hmm," the uniform replies, bobbing his head lazily. "Over there," he says, nodding to a young Hispanic couple in their late thirties across the street. "Franklin's taking their statements now."

"Guess we'd better get to talking, then," Carter says while he stands back up. "We'll check out that second vic after we hear from them." Amara nods. The pair of them cross back under the tape together. They make their way toward the couple standing on the sidewalk. The man and woman are flanked by two officers and a squad car.

The man is heavyset, wearing a dark gray hoodie and jeans. He has short, gelled hair. The woman is wearing black leggings and a sweatshirt. "Morning," Carter greets them as he flashes his badge.

"Good morning," the man replies.

"I'm Detective Murphy," he tells him. "This is my partner, Detective Cruz. We'd like to ask you a few questions if that's all right." The man nods.

Carter takes a small notepad from his pocket and flips to a blank page. "So, you're the ones who called it in?"

The man hesitates before responding. "Yeah. We both saw it. I tried to help after the guy left, but it was too late, so we just waited for the cops to show."

"What did you see exactly?" Amara follows up.

"Not much," the man answers. "We were just coming home. Heard all this screaming. Then I saw a man on top of that one," he says, nodding toward Henry's corpse. "Looked like he stabbed him, then just kept bashing his head against the pavement."

"What'd he look like?" Amara questions.

"We couldn't really see his face," the woman answers, half-shrugging. "Just that he was white. Long dark hair. Wore all black."

"Would you be willing to come down to the station?" Amara asks. "Might help us if you could work with a sketch artist."

"Can't say how much help we'll be, but sure," the woman replies with a tired smile.

A silver Mercedes pulls up next to their parked Crown Victoria. "Look who it is," Amara observes, nodding toward the car. Carter turns his head and watches the vehicle as it parks. The door opens and Katherine steps out.

"All right, uh, thank you," Carter tells the witnesses. "We appreciate your help. These officers will escort you to the station, and I'll follow up with you soon." He nods, then turns around. "Let's see what she wants," he tells Amara. They begin walking toward Katherine, who is standing on the sidewalk with her arms folded.

"Morning, ma'am. How can we help you?" Carter greets her as he steps under the caution tape. She's standing rigidly with her mouth open as she stares down at Henry's corpse. Carter's words don't register with her at first. Katherine is frozen in horror by the lifeless body she knew so recently. "Ma'am..." he repeats, trying to draw her gaze.

Katherine seems startled by the detective's sudden appearance. She turns to him and shakes her head while a tear streams down her cheek; she wipes it off quickly. Katherine sniffles once, then clears her throat, and collects herself. "What do we know so far?" she asks.

Carter and Amara exchange uncertain glances. "Not much at this point," he answers, looking back at her. "We just got to the scene ourselves. Spoke to a couple of witnesses who didn't see much."

"I..." She pauses and takes a deep breath. "I can't believe this. I'd just seen him."

"When?" Amara questions.

"Uh, just a few hours ago. I think we left right before midnight," Katherine answers, shaking her head. She can't stop looking down at the body.

"Where were you?" Amara asks.

"The Tennessee Tavern. We'd just had a few drinks together. He'd won a big murder case earlier; it was that crazy guy who killed his wife."

"Were you with anyone? Or did you notice anyone watching you?"

Katherine sniffles again and wipes her eyes dry before responding. "No...it was just us. It was supposed to be an office thing, but a few people canceled."

Amara gazes at her curiously. "So, no one suspicious, then?"

Katherine shakes her head for a few seconds. "No…" she says finally.

"What all was he working on?" Carter asks her. "We may need to rule out a few people from recent cases."

Katherine thinks for a moment before responding. "A rape case, a couple burglaries, a robbery. A few possessions."

"That's it?"

"Yeah, that's it. He'd just cleared two big cases," Katherine says, sighing. "But listen, I've got to go…I have to call the DA and tell him about this."

"Okay, just let us know if you think of anything else," Carter tells her.

Katherine nods her head and then begins walking away.

"Not really the kind of thing you'd kill for, is it?" he says once she's out of earshot.

Amara doesn't respond. She's looking down at Henry's body, grimacing at his mangled face. "Maybe it had something to do with the Asher case…"

Carter grunts. "In case you forgot, he's dead," he says plainly.

"I know that," she replies, cutting her eyes at him. "I meant someone connected to him, inspired by him." She squats down next to the body to get a better look.

"Well, you could be onto something there. Cases like his…they always tend to bring the freaks out."

"Something this vicious seems personal. And it just feels familiar," she says, rising from the ground.

"Maybe. But for now, my money's on it being something from his private life. We'll dump his phone records, and hopefully, that'll give us a start."

Carter begins hacking while he clears his throat. He spits on the ground before reaching inside his coat pocket. Then he takes out a pack of nicotine gum and pops a piece into his mouth.

"You all right there?" Amara asks with a slight look of disgust.

"Never better. Come on, let's check out that other body." The pair of them walk to it.

They're standing over the second victim when a new officer approaches. "Hey, looks like they found his car," he says, pointing over at Henry.

"Where was it?" Amara questions.

"Couple of miles away. Off Branston and Third. It was torched in the middle of the road. They're still putting it out now."

"Goddamn..." Carter says, looking to his partner. "Let's get a quick look here, and then we'll head it out and see it."

Chapter Seven

I.

Downtown Atlanta

January 28, 2025

11:00 p.m.

I'm amazed at how quickly I heal now, how invulnerable I've become. The killing, it's made me stronger—I can feel it in my bones. My bloody service has been rewarded, and every drop shed has made me better than before.

I'm downtown now, stalking little Miss Mollie through the streets. She's wearing a leather jacket, a short black skirt, torn fishnet stockings, and a matching shirt with cutouts. She's not wearing her hair down this time. No, Mollie's found a new way to obscure my little reminder. She's covered it with a rose tattoo. And it's a shame, really, because you can hardly tell the mark is there now.

The moon and stars above sparkle with blood and promise; the deep blues of the night sky are an ocean of possibility. We're walking together through the darkness, she and I. I'm hot on her trail and have been for some time. I've been following her for days now.

Mollie has fallen quite low, the poor thing. I suppose she couldn't deal with what happened between us. Before, she'd been in college, well on her way to becoming a productive citizen. And now, she's taken to selling herself for a quick fix. I've seen her do it twice.

I can't help but delight in the depths to which she's fallen. There's always something so touching about the loss of one's humanity. To see it scurry, chased away by hungry rats. But I mustn't lose myself too much in these pleasing developments. For there is work to be done, and I am on the clock.

I skulk and hide in the shadows before following her down a dark alleyway. I peek my head around the corner. Beggars and derelicts litter the walls; they sit atop cardboard boxes and lean against overstuffed dumpsters. A fire burns in a metal trashcan as an elderly bearded man warms his hands over it.

Mollie passes them by without concern. She makes her way toward the end of the alley. It's a dead end, enshrouded by brick and mortar. A man sits at the bottom of the concrete steps in front of a doorway at the end. He's scrolling on his phone as she approaches. They make a quick transaction with hushed voices. Mollie puts the little baggie in her coat pocket as she starts heading back down the alleyway again.

Once I see her heading my way, I pop my head back around the corner. She may not recognize me, but I don't want to give myself away. Not yet. As she emerges from the alley, she takes a left turn, not bothering to mind her surroundings. I'm only about ten feet away, leaning against the brick wall, and grinning.

As Mollie starts making her way down the sidewalk, I follow behind her casually. I put my hands in my jacket pockets while I study her every move.

Mollie continues walking for another block; it's a lazy, half-stumbling kind of pace. And all the while, I can see her, taste her, *smell* her. But she does not feel my presence. She approaches a bar in a seedy part of town. The red neon from the sign above reflects off her face as she heads inside. I wait by the entrance and glance around, giving her a few seconds to get ahead.

Then I walk inside and take in my surroundings. The lights are dim; most of them are confined to the bar and only a few hang overhead elsewhere. It's lightly crowded. I can see that Mollie's made her way up to the bar and is now ordering a drink.

A large tan bouncer is sitting near the entrance with his arms folded. The man must weigh three hundred pounds at least. He's wearing all black, and his head is shaved. He stares at me while sitting atop his metal barstool. I don't care to draw his attention. What to do? I wonder as I scan the small establishment. *Ah, I know...*

I make my way toward the bathroom. It's only a matter of time before she finds her way there, especially considering her recent purchase. And if not, I know where I'll find her again. I come to the bathroom door, glance around, and then walk inside.

The small, cramped room reeks of shit. Its filthy tile walls are broken and chipped in places. There's a small crack in the corner of the mirror. My feet stick to the floor with every step. I open one of the stalls and glance down. And there's our culprit: the toilet is filled to the brim with dirty water and floating excrement. I try flushing it, but the lever is useless.

There's nothing to do, then, but turn around and wait. I close the door and take a seat on the commode. I watch eagerly through the small crevice at the edge of the door. A woman in a red dress stumbles inside. She tries to open my stall door at first, but then realizes that it's occupied. "Sorry," she mutters. The woman opens the stall door next to me; she sighs loudly as she sits and begins urinating. It seems to go on for an exceedingly long time. I'm eager for her to finish as I keep my eye fixed upon the door.

About a minute later, the woman is washing her hands and checking her appearance in the broken mirror. She finally departs. I am glad, because I want Mollie all to myself, and we don't need any guest visitors interrupting us. I begin passing the time by carving profanities into the stall divider next to me.

At last, I hear the door opening. And there she is—my prize. I want this to be slow and personal, so I place my knife back inside its sheath. Mollie comes inside, glances in the mirror, and then opens the stall door next to me. She takes a seat, and within seconds, I can hear her sparking a lighter. I smell something burning while I stand up and make my departure.

I close the stall door behind me and walk toward the exit. Then I lean against the wall near the door with my arms folded. I can hear her sighing with relief as she shoots the heroin into her veins. The high is taking a quick hold of her. Mollie's breath becomes tranquil as passing clouds. About half a minute goes by, and I hear her stand up. The lock on her stall clicks, and the door creaks open slowly. I wait for her to emerge.

Mollie walks out, not paying any attention at first. She sets her emptied syringe down on the countertop and then turns the handle on at the faucet. After a few seconds, I come off the wall and lock the bathroom door. She hears the click of the lock and turns her head sharply to the right. Mollie appears startled as her eyes grow wide. She takes a step back and bumps into the wall behind her.

"Hi, Mollie," I greet her in a deep, warm tone. I flash a toothy grin as our eyes meet.

"How...how can you?" she sputters and stammers while her breath grows ragged with fear.

"A deal was made," I tell her calmly. My voice comes as smooth, noxious butter. I begin advancing toward her slowly, gesturing with my arms, and smiling.

She starts digging in her purse for something. I snatch it from her hands and throw it against the wall behind me. Then I place my hands around her throat, pressing her against the wall. Our bodies are pushed tightly together as I breathe a sigh of relief. Her face becomes flush while I press harder upon her throat. Her bloodshot eyes dart aimlessly across the room.

Mollie raises her hands to mine, but she cannot pry them off. She tries kneeing me in the groin, so I press her legs back up against the wall. She grows desperate as she claws at my hands, my face. Finally, she takes a few of those frantic fingers and jams them into my eyes. She digs in, pressing her nail into the socket. I reel back for an instant while she escapes my grasp. Mollie rushes toward the door and reaches for the lock. But before she can turn it, my hands are on her shoulders.

I throw her back violently. She stumbles back a few paces and then falls against the half-opened stall door. She's on the ground now, sitting on her ass, propped up with her hands on the floor. Mollie stares at me and screams loudly; she calls for help and begins trying to stand back up. And it seems that our little game must come to an end.

I lunge toward her, realizing that I must shut her up quickly. My eyes are still burning; I rub them with my right hand as I take hold of her with the left. But my pain diminishes once a simple, artless rage takes over. I catch her while she's on her knees and grab the back of her neck tightly. I take hold with both hands and push her toward the toilet. Mollie's fighting against me with all her strength; she presses her hands hard against the edge of the bowl.

Nonetheless, it's not enough. Her head descends slowly as she starts losing our fight. The shit-filled water grows closer and closer; her face is mere inches away now as she continues screaming. But her shrieks are muted once her head is submerged. The water begins to bubble as she chokes on the contents inside. Her hands flail against the bowl while she struggles against me. I put my full weight down on top of her head as my legs straddle her back. She tries desperately to push her head to the surface. Tries, tries, but all in vain. Mollie's efforts become weaker and weaker as she's further deprived of oxygen.

At last, all her thrashing subsides, and she is set free, gone from this Earth. I let go and stand up slowly with my hands still stretched toward her. There is no movement. Mollie's head floats in the brown liquid, and she remains on her knees.

It looks like the one who got away never really went that far. I breathe heavily and collect myself as a reigning peace surrounds me. Then I look down at my arms. They are covered in vile, human filth. Urine and excrement trickle down to my elbows. I begin to chuckle at the sight of it. But my revelry is cut short by an unwanted intrusion. *Boom, boom, boom!* An angry fist pounds loudly on the other side of the bathroom door.

"The fuck's goin' on in there?" a man's voice thunders.

Fuck. Of course. There's no time to dawdle and there's no space to relish in this moment. I back out of the stall and scan the room around me.

There's no way out. There's a small window near the ceiling, but I'd never be able to squeeze through it. And how would I even get up there?

"Come out now, or I'm calling the cops!" the man on the other side warns.

As I continue glancing around the room, I see Mollie's emptied syringe lying on the counter. *Hello,* dear friend. I smile as I grab it and step cautiously toward the door. More banging comes. The grimy white door moves a little on its hinges with every loud thud. I wait for the pounding to stop and then unlock the door.

Silence follows as I take a few steps back. The large tan bouncer from before throws the door open. He glares at me, taking stock of my shit-covered arms and the syringe in my hand. I giggle as our eyes meet. He stares at me with disgust and then looks down, noticing Mollie's feet hanging out of the opened stall door.

His mouth hangs open for half a second as he realizes what's happened. But he snaps out of it quickly as revulsion sets in. Our eyes lock again after he's taken in the room. He charges toward me, clocking me square on the chin. The blow staggers me, and the man grabs hold of my shoulders. He punches me again. The blow lands on my nose, and within seconds, it begins to bleed.

The big, heaving ogre throws my body like a thin ragdoll. My arms flail as I crash into the mirror. My legs and lower back careen into the countertop. The impact leaves a large, weblike crack down the center of the glass. I nearly fall to my knees, struggling to breathe as I grab the aching spot on my lower back.

But the man's not done. He hoists me up and forces me against the countertop again. He punches me in the gut. While he continues striking me, something takes hold from within. My eyes flash a pale blue as my teeth become razors. The lights flicker, and I welcome the dark aura that engulfs me. As he's rearing back to strike me again, I tackle him to the ground. My strength is superhuman as I clamp my sharpened teeth upon his collar bone.

Blood begins flowing from his shoulder. I can feel my teeth sinking deep into his trapezius muscle. I clench it between my mighty jaws. He wails in agony as I draw back. I look down on him with an animal's vigor. As my pulse slows, I realize that the syringe is still in my hand. A deep bellowing comes from some hidden cavern within me; it's not a sound I recognize, nor one I could repeat. My leonine roar fills the room as I hear someone behind me shriek.

I raise the syringe overhead with both arms. Then I bring it crashing down on the man's face. It sticks deeply in his eye. He screams out in a high pitch. It's a broken cry that doesn't last long; it reaches a quick crescendo and then fades into a dying whimper. I drive the needle further and further down inside, placing both hands atop the plunger.

The needle must have pierced his brain, because the man has instantly stopped flailing and spasming on the floor. His face is frozen in terror, but his arms hang limply by his sides. His head sags as I release the needle from my grasp. And suddenly, I come back to my senses, realizing that I am in a public place, surrounded now by many people. I begin rising from the filthy tile floor as my eyes and teeth return to their natural state.

Reality has crept back into this small bathroom, and I realize that it's time to go. I lean against the wall for support, leaving a large, bloody handprint on the dingy backsplash as I stand up. Then I stumble to the door and see that there's a small crowd of onlookers gathered. They're staring at me. Some are frozen in shock; others gasp in fear as I approach.

I keep my head low and push past the crowd. A man that's mingled in with them tries grabbing me by the arm as I make my way through. I shake him off, then head toward the red sign above the rear exit.

I make my departure and start running through the alley. I'm not sure if anyone is behind me. I don't bother looking, because I won't risk being taken down by a lynch mob. I've accomplished what I came here for, and that's all that matters now.

II.

Fulton County Police Department

January 30, 2025

6:30 p.m.

"Christ, I was really hoping you were wrong..." Carter complains. He rubs his tired eyes, reaches into his breast pocket, and takes out a pair of reading glasses. He's wearing a white dress shirt with the top buttons undone and a pair of wrinkled gray slacks.

"Me too," Amara replies sullenly. She's wearing a white blouse, dark blue slacks, and has a black pistol holstered across her shoulder.

Carter stands up slowly. "Eighteen hours on shift...and it doesn't matter how I roll it around. I can't see how they're not connected. It's got to be a copycat."

"Or maybe he wasn't working alone," she replies.

"Could be. First, it was the prosecutor on his case, now his lead witness, a few incidentals...All killed in a short time span, all in ways that can only described as barbaric."

The pair of them stand in front of a bulletin board with photographs of the victims from the recent string of killings. The room is coated in various shades of gray, from the carpets to the walls. "He even looks like him," Carter says, glancing up at the artist's sketch hanging on the board.

Amara nods and continues staring at the photographs intently. "My question is how the new guy is doing it. I don't see how he could survive that wreck, then chase Adams through the streets, kill him, and still manage to get away."

"And just a few days later, he's drowning Mollie Hamilton in a barroom toilet, and taking on his big ass..." Carter says, pointing to the bouncer's picture. "It takes a special kind of crazy to stab somebody in the eye." The detective shakes his head, looks to the ground, and sighs. He walks over to a large glass window and watches the officers passing by for a moment. They're scurrying about the police station, drinking coffee, escorting suspects, and keeping themselves busy with paperwork. "It feels like it's him all over again. And unfortunately, I don't know how much longer I've got left."

She glances at him curiously. "Thought you weren't supposed to retire for a few more years."

"It's medical," he mutters, still staring out the window absently. "My results came back. Emphysema. Doc said the job will probably be too much on me before long." He waits a few seconds for his words to resonate as she stares at him.

"I...I don't know what to say," she replies.

"Nothing to say," he responds, turning around, and facing her. Carter shrugs. "That's life. Tell you what, though, I'd love to put this shit behind me before I go. I want him wrapped up *first*," he says, pointing to the board. He walks over and stands next to her. "I think we need to start reaching out to everyone involved in the case. No telling who could be next."

Amara glances at Carter and then nods her head uncertainly.

Chapter Eight

I.

Cynthia Hallsley's Apartment

January 30, 2025

8:00 p.m.

Cynthia Hallsley's phone vibrates against a glass table inside of her living room. She's standing in her kitchen, watching the microwave as it heats up a bag of popcorn. She has her hair in a bun and is wearing an oversized T-shirt with gym shorts on underneath. Across the apartment, a toilet flushes inside her hallway bathroom.

James Edwards is washing his hands and checking his teeth in the bathroom mirror. He wipes his hands on a towel that's hung next to the sink. James is wearing a plain white T-shirt with black sweatpants. He fogs up his glasses with his breath and then cleans them with his shirttail. Once he's satisfied with his appearance, James opens the door and steps out into the hallway.

He begins making his way down the hall, passing by a row of Cynthia's family photographs. Then he walks into the kitchen and approaches her from behind. James wraps his arms around her waist as they wait for the popcorn to finish. He raises a hand to her chin and turns her head

136

toward him. They kiss for several seconds before they're interrupted by the intrusive beeping of the microwave. She pulls away, and they smile at one another. As Cynthia pulls the bag out of the microwave, James walks into the living room and sits down on her couch.

Cynthia pours the bag of popcorn into an orange bowl and then makes her way into the living room. The carpets running through her apartment are all a dull gray. The walls are white and adorned with uplifting slogans and tranquil decor. A single lamp on the end table lights up the room, and the television emits dark blue rays from her home screen. Above the television hangs a large portrait of the Virgin Mary; her hands are clasped, and her humble eyes stare with an innocent, pleading expression.

Cynthia's couch is a well-worn red and blue plaid. She takes a seat next to James and snuggles up next to him. James picks up the remote from the end table and starts navigating the menu. He puts his arm around Cynthia, and she leans against his chest, tucking her legs beneath her on the couch.

Cynthia's phone lights up and vibrates a single time on the table. She looks down, sighs, and leans over to grab it. "Hmm...a missed call," she says with an air of boredom in her voice. "Says it's from Atlanta PD. Wonder what that's about."

"It's probably one of those stupid fundraiser things. I get those a lot too," James replies, shoving a handful of popcorn into his mouth.

"Guess so," Cynthia says, tilting her head. "They left a message."

"Come on...you can listen to that later," he complains. "It's scary movie time," James says, flashing a quick smile.

"You're right," Cynthia replies with a light smirk. She leans back on the couch, kisses him on the cheek, and nestles against his chest again.

"You ready?" James asks mischievously, arching his eyebrows several times.

"So scary…" she answers in a playful tone.

James smiles and presses play. "You're going to love my new sound system. It's amazing."

A portentous orchestra begins playing as the camera pans across a gloomy graveyard. The volume is thunderous. As the camera paces through the darkened cemetery, it settles upon a scene with six hooded figures. They're wearing dark brown robes with ropes tied around the waist. Their faces are obscured, and their heads are held low.

The figures approach from all sides and surround a woman who is stretched upon an altar. She's bound by hand and foot to the stone beneath her. Her blonde hair is a tangled mess. The woman's face is scratched and bloodied, and her clothes are torn. One of the robed figures stands behind her. Two more approach on either side, and the last halts in front of her. They each plant a flaming torch in the ground near the altar; it forms a burning pentagram from above.

The woman is struggling against her bondage as one of the figures draws a thick leather-bound book from his robe. He begins reading a long passage aloud in Latin. The man is flipping through the pages; each of them depicts a scene of feral demons flying above the earth and tormenting the inhabitants below.

"By the power of Satan, we sacrifice this pure, untainted flesh. Prince of Darkness, honor us, and release your unholy masses!" the man proclaims. He closes the book and then tucks it back under his robe. He stares down at the bound, forlorn woman as a deep, ominous bass fills the room through the booming speakers.

The other five figures begin stabbing the woman over and over again. She screams as the knives plunge in and out of her body from all sides. The camera draws closer as she takes her final breath. The figures stand in silence for a moment. Then the torch's flames reach a new height, filling the screen with radiant light as the sound of splitting earth plays throughout. The robed man in front begins cackling with his arms outstretched while he looks up to the sky.

A single bolt of lightning strikes the ground near them. The man stares at the spot in anticipation. A gray hand emerges from the earth, reaching its fingers toward the sky above. A second hand pops out several feet away from it. A third. A fourth. Hands begin sprouting all over the graveyard as the man becomes entranced by the unfolding events. Bodies begin emerging from the dirt; their hideous, gaunt faces are insatiably murderous. The man smiles with yellow teeth and nods as large, bloody letters overtake the screen.

"Curse of the Satanic Zombies?" Cynthia questions. "Really, this is what you picked?"

James snickers to himself as he cuts his eyes to her. "It's a classic. Just give it a chance."

The movie continues playing, but Cynthia's attention is focused elsewhere. She continues glancing at her phone between the violent segments unfolding on the screen. "I'll be right back," she tells James.

Cynthia stands up and grabs her phone from the table. "Do you want me to pause it?" he asks, glancing up at her.

She looks at the screen and then back at him. "No, that's okay," she replies, chuckling under her breath.

Cynthia walks down the hallway toward her master bath. After closing the door, she checks her reflection in the mirror. She sighs while adjusting her hair. "I hate these stupid movies," she grumbles. Cynthia sits on the toilet, then unlocks her phone. She scrolls a moment before bringing it to her ear.

"Good evening, Ms. Hallsley," Carter's voicemail greets her. "It's Detective Murphy, one of the investigators on the Asher case. I'm calling on a pretty urgent matter. If you could give me a call back as soon as you get this, I'd appreciate it. I have some important things to discuss with you. The number is…" Cynthia pulls the phone from her ear and studies it with concern. She remains there for several seconds, dissecting the message she'd just received.

Then Cynthia stands up, goes to the sink, and washes her hands. As she looks in the mirror, she hears a loud scream coming from the next room. Cynthia turns her head and stares at the door, trying to listen through it. A loud orchestra plays, and she can hear the groans and cries of the possessed zombies on film. She shakes her head and rolls her eyes as she opens the bathroom door.

The apartment is filled with screeching cries while Cynthia begins heading down the hallway. She has her phone in her hand still, and she's reading the transcribed message from Carter as she walks along. "Hey, babe…" Cynthia says while walking into the living room. "That call was from that detective on the case." She looks up, noticing that James is no longer seated on the couch.

Cynthia scans the room with some confusion. She's still holding her phone as she peeks her head over the bar and peers into the kitchen. She glances at the front door and sees that it's still locked with the chain secured as well. Then Cynthia looks down the hall, noticing that the lights are off in both the second bathroom and guest room.

Someone screams loudly on the film playing beside her. Cynthia appears startled as she turns around, sighs, and picks up the remote from the living room table. Then she turns off the television.

"*Okay*, very funny," she says. "Joke's over…I need to talk to you." Irksome silence follows. Cynthia waits several seconds longer and then sticks her head out impatiently. "James!" she calls. "Would you just come out? We're not watching these stupid movies anymore if you keep playing games." Cynthia waits a few more seconds for his response. Then she glances around the apartment, calling him a jerk under her breath.

Cynthia walks toward the guest bathroom. She turns the light on and takes a hard look at the shower curtain. Her expression tightens while she steps toward it. She rips the curtain open but finds nothing behind it. Her agitation grows as she calls his name again. "James!" She waits. "This isn't funny," Cynthia complains. She turns and glances past the doorway.

Then Cynthia heads out of the bathroom and starts walking down the hallway. She passes the living room and places her hand on the bedroom doorknob. But before she can turn the handle, she hears a faint click on the other side of the apartment. All the lights go out. Cynthia lets go of the door's handle and peers through the darkness toward the guest bedroom.

She walks a few paces to the living room and tries the light switch on the wall. She flips it several times, but the switch does nothing. Near silence fills the apartment around her as she shakes her head; only the sounds of the insects and birds outside provide her any comfort. "I can hear you in there messing with the breaker," Cynthia chides. "James!" she calls again, extending her head to see into the spare room as she advances toward it.

Cynthia stops in the center of the living room and unlocks her phone. She shines its light upon the kitchen countertop. A large white candle in a decorative glass sits next to a book of matches. She picks up the matchbook, strikes one, and lights the candle. The dim light stretches out into the room as she takes hold of it.

Cynthia thinks for a moment as she leans against the countertop. She scrolls through her phone, goes into her contacts, then calls James. Cynthia puts the phone to her ear and waits while it starts ringing.

Then she pulls the phone away and listens to her surroundings. She can hear a faint buzzing coming from the guest bedroom. "Mm-hmm…" she grunts with some satisfaction. "Big, dumb idiot." The phone continues ringing a moment longer before going to James' voicemail.

Cynthia drops the call and then puts the phone back into her pocket. She holds the candle near her chest as she begins making her way down the hall toward the guest bedroom. "I know you're in there," she calls out. "I could hear your phone ringing from here…" She pauses mid-sentence when she reaches the doorway.

As the sparse candlelight fills the room, Cynthia can see a figure sitting at a desk by the window. He faces away from her. A few seconds pass before she calls his name again, "James!" She shakes her head. "Okay, you got me." A few more seconds pass in eerie silence. She steps further into the room, shining her light in front of her.

But as she draws closer, she finds the figure unfamiliar. She sees my long hair draped across my shoulders; my head is bent low. I am carving my name into the wood of the desk when I glance up at her. A smile spreads across my face as our eyes meet in the dim light.

II.

Cynthia Hallsley's Residence

January 30, 2025

8:30 p.m.

"So quick to condemn…so slow to understand," I tell her in a low, flat tone as I turn toward her in my chair. Cynthia's candlelight illuminates my face, and it seems her suspicions are confirmed immediately. Her shock is apparent as she mindlessly staggers back toward the doorway.

Cynthia freezes in place. It's as if something is blocking her retreat; all she can do is stare at me like a stationary deer in front of moving headlights. "We all have our purpose in life, Cynthia," I say, rising from my seat. "And mine is merely different than yours."

Her eyes flutter as she seems to suddenly comprehend the danger she's in. Cynthia flees the room in a panic. "Did that occur to you?!" I call after her. I swipe my arm across the desk, shoving a lamp and a computer onto the floor. "Does anything *ever* occur to you?!" I head to the bedroom door and start making my way down the hallway after her.

Cynthia makes it to the front door as I'm pacing down the hall, holding the knife by my side. A dark cloud forms around her as she stands by the door, fumbling with the chain up top. She releases the chain and turns the deadbolt. Her hand shakes while she holds the candle and tries pulling on the doorknob. It's unlocked now, but when she tugs against the knob, the door still refuses to open.

I can't help but giggle at the sight of her helpless jerking and wrenching as she attempts to open the door. The fog surrounding her is so dark and dense that her light barely pierces it. It hangs around her, ominous and enshrouding. I stroll leisurely down the hallway and place my hand against the kitchen bar as I lay my eyes upon her. My gaze is fixed as I begin tapping my ring against the laminate.

Cynthia becomes frantic once she realizes that the door won't budge. Her head vacillates between the door and me as I continue meandering toward her. I'm at the end of her countertop, resting my hand on the edge, watching her while she makes her decision.

She turns toward me, wild-eyed and desperate. I widen my eyes and gasp in mockery of her fear. She throws her candle at me. I move deftly out of the way, and the candle crashes against a cabinet door behind me. Glass and melted wax fall to the counter below.

Cynthia darts past me and then heads down the hallway toward her bedroom. I watch her calmly as she scampers away and throws open the door. Inside, it's dim, and the blinds are half-turned; only feeble streams of blue light creep inside the room. Cynthia slams the door behind her and locks it. Then she pulls out her cell phone and starts dialing 9-1-1.

"9-1-1, what's your emergency?" a woman's voice answers.

"There's a man in my house!" Cynthia exclaims. "He's trying to kill me!"

"Okay, ma'am, try to remain calm. I'll send the police immediately. Can you tell me your address?"

As Cynthia turns from the door, she's taken aback by what she discovers. Still clenching the phone in her hand, her terror grows when she sees James lying upon the bed. Her jaw begins to tremble as she takes a step toward him with her arm outstretched. Tears start flowing from her eyes while she stares at her boyfriend in disbelief. James' right arm is severed; it's lying next to him on the floor. His legs hang off the edge of the bed as he lies there stationary.

As Cynthia approaches, James opens one eye, groaning, and reaching his remaining arm toward her. He tries sitting up at first but finds himself powerless. Still dazed, the man stares at her with a simple, pleading expression. He begins muttering something to her, but she can't hear what he's saying, because I am now at the door, rattling away. As I push the door and twist the handle, I can hear her scream loudly on the other side.

Cynthia puts the phone up to her chest and looks around the room like a scared, caged animal. The entire apartment falls silent. I press my ear up to the door and listen. The only sound that comes forth is the nearly muted voice of the operator on the other end of the line.

With nowhere left to run, Cynthia rushes to her closet. It's a white double door with small shutters on the front. She pulls one side open and quickly closes it behind her. Then she sits on the floor and peers out of the small openings from the shutters.

It suddenly occurs to her that she's still clutching onto the phone. Cynthia looks down and then holds it up to her ear. She breathes a sigh of relief when she hears the operator telling her that they've traced her location, and that the police will be there shortly.

I continue rattling the door for another few seconds before it opens with a faint click. The cheap lock has given way. Then I walk inside and draw a breath of fresh air. I can see that James is still sprawled out on the bed where I left him. I smile and give a friendly wave as he looks at me in defeat.

Inside the closet, Cynthia holds the phone to her chest again and dares not breathe for fear of giving herself away. Sweet, blissful silence is all that exists for several seconds. I take it in as I admire the dismembered man laid out before me. He tries to sit up but can't muster the strength. I watch his feeble attempts as I walk closer, hovering over his helpless body.

"Cynthia..." James mutters, reaching his shaky arm toward me.

I click my tongue several times while I stare at James with amusement. I walk closer and wag the knife in front of his face. Then I raise it quickly and stab him in the shoulder; he cries out in pain. I start screaming alongside him, matching his pain with my pleasure.

Then I press the blade's handle down with both hands, exerting myself as I drive it in deep. James' rally fades into a dying whimper. He begins sobbing quietly. I draw the blade out and start stabbing him several more times, quickly now, driving each thrust in and out with little effort.

I stab him in the chest. I stab him in the arms. I stab him in the neck. And as I witness the life vanishing from his eyes, I stab him in the middle of his forehead. The knife juts out as blood pours from the open wound. It flows and pools onto the bedspread beneath him.

Then I draw the blade from his wound and take a step back. I blow the hair out of my face and twist my hips while I catch my breath, stretching my neck from side to side. I'm feeling quite limber now. My body feels relaxed as a gentle peace falls over me.

Cynthia is behind the closet door, cowering in fear as she stares through the shudders. Her unblinking eyes have watched it all. She's watched her boyfriend die, realizing that there's nothing to be done. And there's a special solace I take in that—when the suffering of one bleeds onto another. The growing malice compounds and swirls, giving me more sustenance than I can handle. My eyes gleam like diamonds in the dark as I take it all in.

The feeling of danger slithers back into the closet with Cynthia once she realizes that she's alone inside the room now, and that there's no longer anything else taking my attention from her. She leans back from the shudders while her breath quickens. Her back is against the wall as hopelessness envelops her. Cynthia appears dazed while she turns her head gently, observing all her surroundings.

Beside her on a low shelf, there's a wooden crucifix next a few framed pictures. It's about six inches long, dark and faded. Her breath grows ragged when she reaches out and grabs it. She clutches it next to her chest while she holds the phone there. Cynthia stares through the door for a few seconds with her mouth hanging open. She closes her eyes and begins mouthing a silent prayer.

Cynthia begs. Begs for me to be gone from this place. Begs to be free of this haunting presence. She stares into the thins rays of light coming through her shutters. She's frozen in the depths of darkness as desolation forms around her.

But her time has come. There can be no more dithering games. I open the double doors slowly. They creak as I pull them apart and reveal her presence; she's shaking and cowering on the floor. "No! No, please!" Cynthia begs. I tilt my head as I drag the blade across my cheek. I'm towering over her now; my hungry eyes stare deeply into hers.

I lunge toward Cynthia and grab her by the collar of her shirt. I wrench her from her seated position and force her onto her feet again. She's jerking wildly, and it causes her to drop her phone onto the floor. Its blue light illuminates the room as she tries to get away from me, but my grip is built of stone. My head bobs lightly in response to all her jostling, but my heart doesn't quicken in the slightest. I stare at her calmly as my hair enshrouds half my face.

Then I move my hands up to her neck and squeeze tightly. Cynthia's eyes bulge as she tries to pry my fingers from her throat. With great force, I turn and press her against the wall. My left hand is wrapped like a coil around her neck as I stab her in the stomach with my right. She's not quite able to scream, but a loud whimper escapes her throat as the blade enters her flesh. I pull the knife out, raise it above my head, and stab her just below the collar bone. My expression is vacant while I stare into her wandering eyes.

My hand's still gripped around Cynthia's neck when I pull the knife out slowly. She snivels as I continue pressing her against the wall. I hold her there a moment longer, then I release her throat, and press that hand against her shoulder to keep her pinned in place.

Cynthia begins sobbing with her eyes closed. She shrinks in fear as I press against her. Then she starts muttering something under her breath in Spanish. I can't speak the language, but I can tell that she's praying. "Shut up," I tell her. I raise my hand to her chin and force her to look at me. "Shut your fucking mouth and look at me!"

Her eyes creep open one at a time. I clench her jaw tightly with my fingers, and it scrunches up her face. "It's time," I tell her, nodding my head as I stare with a razor's promise. I raise the knife overhead, but as I do, she blurts something out in Spanish and raises the crucifix in front of her. She clutches it tightly, extending the wood forward.

"Gahhhh!" I cry out. "My arm!"

Pain radiates from my right shoulder down to my fingertips. It starts spreading throughout my entire body like virulent sickness. The contagion takes me over, and I am forced down to one knee. I howl in pain as I clutch my shoulder, kneeling upon the floor. My eyes glow a penetrating blue that brightens the room like a moonlit sky. My teeth are sharpened metal as my jaw hangs open. Blood mixes with saliva; it covers my lips and runs onto the floor.

Cynthia slumps against the wall, staring at me in bewilderment. She examines the crucifix and then cuts her eyes toward me again. I reach my arm out to grab her, but I nearly fall over in the process. I catch myself on both knees and stare at her in strained delirium. My vision is hazy. Blood pours from my shoulder as smoke rises from a forgotten wound.

I drag myself toward Cynthia and reach my arm out again. Frantically, I try to grab her. The frightened woman is still panting while she catches her breath. She raises a blood-soaked hand to her reddened throat and takes a step toward the door. Cynthia holds the crucifix in front of her and repeats the same words as before.

I cry out; it comes louder as the pain intensifies. I drop the knife involuntarily, and I am brought low to all fours. My elbows are on the carpet and my hands clutch my head tightly as I writhe in agony. The blood from my shoulder begins pooling onto her gray carpet. The foul smoke continues rising; it hangs in the room like a thin cloud of ashes.

"You miserable bitch!" I scream angrily. I can't turn my head or even look at her. My face grates against the fibers of the carpet. I feel a great weight pressing me down, and I'm completely unable to move.

Suddenly, I am transplanted. I quickly find myself in a different place and time. I'm back at the courthouse now, and I'm wearing my bright orange jumpsuit. My hands are shackled in front, but I hold a pistol in between them. I see the judge fleeing the courtroom, and I take aim.

My barrel pursues the old man as he bolts toward the exit. A shot rings out, but nothing happens for several seconds. I am held in dreamlike suspense before a bullet lodges into my shoulder and puts me off balance.

I scream in pain as I watch the man escape. Then I turn with bitter resignation. And there she is: the cause of all my pain, past and present. Our eyes meet. Amara stares down her barrel, watching my movements tensely. I fall to the floor before I'm able to return fire. As they begin subduing me, I am brought back to reality by the force of their blows.

Once I come back to my senses, I spot Cynthia fleeing the bedroom. I reach my arm out in a pathetic attempt to grab her ankle, but I do not come close to grasping my target. Lying on the floor, enfeebled, it occurs to me that my current situation rings all too familiar. I collapse to the ground with my cheek pressed against the carpet.

Cynthia exits the room and quickly makes it to the front door. It's still dark inside her apartment with the power off, but the black mass from before has vanished. She turns the knob, finding it free of its former oppression, and opens the door. Cynthia rushes down the hallway, running as fast as she can with the crucifix still clutched tightly in her hand.

Chapter Nine

I.

Mr. Fatty's BBQ

February 2, 2025

1:15 p.m.

"I'm just glad we warned the judge in time. I'm sure he falls on the roster somewhere," Carter mutters while raising a pork sandwich to his lips. "It's too bad about James Edwards. Looked like a hard way to go. Never seen somebody go after the jury before."

Amara leans back in her chair at the table, staring off pensively. The pair of them are outside of a downtown restaurant, sitting beneath a red umbrella. They're both wearing dark suits. Amara sits with her legs crossed and her hands in her lap, paying little attention to her meal.

"You gonna eat those?" Carter asks, nodding toward her basket of fries. Amara shrugs and slides it to him.

Carter begins picking fries from the basket. "So, what's on your mind?"

"Just wish we could have reached her in time," Amara says, watching as a young couple crosses through an intersection together.

"Well, we tried." Carter pauses for a moment and then clears his throat. "Gave her a call, remember?" He begins eating again. "Tried James Edwards too. Can't help it if folks don't answer."

Amara cuts her eyes at him. She starts to reply but decides against it as she studies the busy scenery ahead.

"There was no way of knowing who he'd strike next, and we reached out to everybody we could. The jurors didn't even seem that likely. It wasn't public information."

"Had to be someone inside that courtroom, then," she counters. "Someone who'd seen their faces."

"Yeah," Carter replies, nodding his head as he probes the possibility. "What time is she supposed to meet us here?" He looks down at his watch and raises an eyebrow.

"About 1:30. She told me she had something to share with us."

"Something not in her statement?" he asks, flipping through a brown folder on the table as he continues eating.

"Guess so."

"It's hard to figure," Carter says, shaking his head as he looks through the crime scene photographs. "How could one man have taken Edwards from the living room, cut his arm off, and then gotten back on the other side of the apartment? And all that before she even got out of the bathroom. It makes no sense."

"I don't know. But she only saw one man."

"And don't you think he'd be screaming like hell through all that?"

Amara's phone vibrates on the table. She looks down at it before responding, "She, uh, said they were watching a really loud movie."

"Hmm. Is that her?"

"Yeah, she just pulled up."

A moment of silence passes between them as they await Cynthia's arrival. Their eyes shift toward her once she parks near the curb and steps out of her car. She's wearing a black dress and sunglasses, walking with her head down. She moves slowly and appears bothered by her injuries.

"Afternoon, Ms. Hallsley," Carter greets her.

Cynthia smiles meekly and then eases herself into the seat next to Amara. "Thank you for meeting me," she says.

"Of course," Amara replies. "What was it that you had to share?" She smiles without showing her teeth and joins her hands together on the table.

Cynthia looks down and collects her thoughts for a moment. She struggles to find the words. "There was something...that I didn't think anyone would believe."

Carter purses his lips. "Try us," he says, welcoming her with his gaze.

After a moment's hesitation, Cynthia finally replies, "That night—I think there was, I don't know, some kind of witchcraft. It was something evil." Her words come with unhidden trepidation as she stares at the table.

"What do you mean?" Amara questions.

"I couldn't tell the officers when they came. I knew they'd think I was crazy," she replies, taking her sunglasses off and putting them on the table. "It sounds ridiculous when I think about it, when I say it out loud." Cynthia glances into the distance, examining a pedestrian across the street. "But I know what I saw."

"What did you see?" Carter presses.

"It wasn't just what I saw, it was how it felt," she says, shaking her head. "Like something that couldn't be real. Something I wasn't sure could exist here. He...wasn't human. He couldn't have been."

Carter sighs quietly and then looks down before exchanging glances with his partner.

"It's normal to feel that way," Amara responds. "Whoever did this to you was a monster; he was less than human."

"You don't understand," Cynthia pushes back. "He had teeth that no man could have. His eyes were glowing. And when I tried to get out, something was there, like it was stopping me from leaving. It hung like a cloud, a dark cloud of bad energy." Cynthia sniffles and then wipes her eye. "My grandmother, she lived for the church, and it was just like all those things she'd warned me about growing up."

The detectives stare at Cynthia with some confusion as they wait for her to continue. "I know you probably think I imagined it. That it's the grief talking or it's just some way of dealing with what happened." She gazes into both their eyes. "But I did hurt him, and that's the only reason I got away, I know it."

"You managed to fight him off, right?" Carter studies her with curiosity. "That's what we have in your statement here."

Cynthia reaches inside her purse. She takes out the wooden crucifix and sets it on the table. "With this," she says, looking down at it somberly. "He was invincible. Nothing I did could stop him. He was just toying with me until he saw it."

Carter and Amara exchange dubious glances. The constant sounds of the bustling city seem to isolate them as the trio studies the artifact upon the table.

"Tell me more," Amara replies as she gazes up at Cynthia.

II.

Outside of Raven and the Fairy Metaphysical Shop
February 3, 2025
12:30 p.m.

"You're actually considering this?" Carter questions. He curls his lip and scratches his neck. "Like, for real?"

"I think it's worth checking out. We don't have any other leads, anyway," Amara replies, arching her eyebrows. She smiles mischievously. "Come on, old man."

It's a cool winter day out. The sun is masked behind a blanket of thin, gray clouds that move slowly across the sky. The pair of them are dressed warmly as they walk together down the sidewalk.

"Dragging my ass to some *hoodoo magic shop*," Carter complains. The two detectives stop near the doorway of an aging three-story brick building. It's a small shop on the corner next to a convenience store and a derelict mattress shop. The rustic brown sign above them reads, "Raven and the Fairy."

"I ain't never seen a murder get solved by witchcraft. Never. Not once," he continues.

"I'm not saying it's magic or witchcraft. But he might help us make sense of all this. Who knows, the perp might have come in once or twice himself. So quit whining." She smiles again and gestures with her hand toward the door. "Age before beauty."

"Hmmph," he grunts. Carter opens the door and then walks inside, muttering to himself, "Age before beauty...lucky I don't write your ass up for insubordination."

Amara laughs quietly to herself as she walks in behind him.

A bell fastened to the door jingles as they enter. Carter purses his lips and glances around the shop incredulously with his hands in his pockets.

"Hello," Amara calls out. She tilts her head to see around a corner. "Is anyone here?"

She gazes over at Carter. He shrugs and says, "Might as well look around."

There are several dark brown shelves to the left. Cobwebs have formed in many of their corners, and a thin layer of dust runs throughout. Scarce sunlight creeps into the room through the half-opened curtains on the side opposite the register; the thin rays stretch across the store. The dim light fixture above barely adds anything at all. As they walk further into the store, fretful cockroaches scurry into their dark corners. Smoke fills the room with thin clouds coming from a burning incense holder near the register.

Carter scowls and then clears his throat. "God, that stinks," he complains. "Who would work here?"

Amara cuts her eyes at him and shakes her head.

"Somebody weird, I'll bet," he follows up, nodding his head. "You just watch."

"Uh-huh," she acknowledges.

The store's register is near the center of the room on the right side. Behind it, there is an aged rectangular altar. It's set on the counter behind the register with a large display around it. It has a black cloth upon the wood with a sun with a split-face, surrounded by little stars and the symbols of the zodiac; a smaller shelf rests upon the altar with a cast iron mortar and pestle on the right and a golden chalice on the left. Little necklaces and jewelry hang in a display next to a collection of colorful stones and crystals by the register.

To the right of the register is an opening that leads into another part of the store. They walk past it and glance around to see if anyone is inside. Seeing no one, they look ahead and spot another display in the corner. There are small wooden boxes for sale with little moons etched in the center. Assorted tinctures and herbs are available in small glass jars. Below them is another altar; it's a rich mahogany with an elaborate pentagram carved into the wood.

They take their time, walking leisurely around the store and studying its contents. Amara walks toward the first row of shelves; Carter follows behind her reluctantly. She begins perusing some of the items on the dust-laden boards. There are several Ouija boards of various sizes. A few daggers with intricate designs are on display with a little card in front that reads, *"Sacred athame."* The collection of incense reads in alphabetical order, from aloeswood to rosemary.

After Amara finishes examining the first row, she walks down the line of shelves and crosses into the second. Candles, tarot decks, and books of tea leaves and fortune telling surround her on either side. She begins reading their titles as she walks slowly down the line. Carter has lost all interest by now; he gazes out the window in the center of the room, peering out the half-drawn curtain.

"Hey, I think maybe I've found something here..." Amara calls out.

Carter grunts and continues peering out the window for a moment. He takes his time making his way toward her. Amara is now squatting near the bottom shelf, placing her finger beneath a section that reads, "Satanic Witchcraft." She pulls a black leather-bound book from the bottom shelf.

"The Serpent's Call: An Introduction to Black Magic," Amara says, reading the title aloud. She glances over her shoulder and sees her partner approaching. Amara opens the book, stands up, and begins thumbing through it carefully. She glides her finger gently across the pages as she studies the images within: horned creatures devour screaming victims, apparitions emerge from sacred text, and unholy penitents perform black rituals with their heads bowed in deference. Amara skims through the section headings; she runs her finger over the portions on Satanic pacts and demonic apparitions.

"What you got there?" Carter questions as he stands over Amara's shoulder; he begins studying the pages alongside her.

"I'm not sure yet," Amara replies. She's lost in the pages as she studies them one by one. She's toward the end of the book when she sees a large heading spelled out in some ancient, elaborate font. "Banishing Evil Entities," it reads. Carter loses focus and starts examining the shelves nearby. Amara repeats the ritual's name under her breath as though she were held in some sort of dull trance.

But before Amara can study the pages further, she hears the sound of footsteps approaching. "Good afternoon, Detectives," a man's gruff voice greets them. "I've been expecting you."

III.

Raven and the Fairy Metaphysical Shop
February 3, 2025
12:45 p.m.

A dark-skinned man is standing several feet away at the end of the shelves. He's wearing black slacks and a half-buttoned black shirt. The man has long dreadlocks that hang low to his hips. He folds his arms as he leans against a nearby shelf. A sly smile forms on his lips as they all exchange glances with one another. "It's something dark...from your past, isn't it?" he asks with malevolent confidence. "Perhaps I could grant you protection?"

"Are you the owner?" Amara questions, eyeing the man suspiciously.

The man hides his teeth, but his smile widens. He looks around the storefront with measured patience, taking ample time to respond. "I am," he replies. "My name's Rakim Jabari. And what may I help you with?"

Amara glances over her shoulder at Carter and then closes the book with an air of uncertainty. "We're looking for information," she begins, shifting her gaze toward the shop owner. "There's a case we're working on. It...seems to involve the occult."

"You've come to the right place, then," he answers in a friendly tone, arching his eyebrows.

"We want to know if you can tell us about some of these symbols," Carter interjects. He comes toward the man with a thin brown folder in hand. He stops in front of Rakim, opens the folder, and thumbs through a few of the papers and images inside. He sniffs loudly as he picks a few of them out. "Do any of these look familiar to you?" Carter asks, handing the man several printouts of crime scene images.

Rakim studies them for several seconds in silence. He examines each image slowly, raising his eyebrows in surprise, and then holding the picture closer. "This one does," he says at last, tapping one of the photographs. "For the others, I may have to consult my sources."

"Your sources, huh?" Carter questions as he chomps on a piece of nicotine gum.

Rakim glances at him disdainfully as he hands the papers back. "Yes..." he replies.

"I was wondering if you could look at something for me," Amara says.

"Of course," he offers cordially.

Amara starts patting her jacket pockets. She appears surprised when she can't find what she's looking for. "I...must have left it in the car," she says, shaking her head in puzzlement.

"What, that cross?" Carter questions.

"Yeah."

"Come on, do we really need that? It's a piece of wood."

"Just give me a minute," she counters. "I'll be right back."

As Amara heads to the entrance, she can hear Carter continuing his line of questioning. "You had anyone strange come by the shop lately, asking about this kind of stuff?"

"No stranger than you," the man replies smugly. "And no, not that I recall."

Carter furrows his brow. Amara smiles to herself as she walks through the door.

IV.

Raven and the Fairy Metaphysical Shop

February 3, 2025

12:55 p.m.

And there I stand, watching the lady detective as she exits. I lean against the brick façade near the entrance of the shop. I'm wearing black sunglasses, staring at the ground when I hear the bell jingle and see her walk through the door.

Leaving so soon? I think to myself. What a pity. No matter, I'll be back for you—I promise. I watch her with a strange affection as she goes.

It's hard to make sense of what happened last time. I have recovered, but it is a wound that may never fully heal. It could come back at any moment. Perhaps I'm not as invulnerable as I first thought. It seems that what weakens my master must weaken me as well. This soft underbelly grates upon my nerves, but I mustn't let it distract from the task at hand. I must simply be more careful, more astute.

I find it difficult to pull myself away, but I must do so. There is work to be done. I watch her with an empty sense of longing while she crosses the road. As Amara walks to the other side, she answers a call on her cell phone and then stops on the sidewalk. And that'll be my cue.

I stand up from the wall and walk inside casually. I keep my head down as I enter the store. Then I glance to my left and pretend not to notice Carter and the shop owner talking to one another. Rakim is pointing down at a large black book as Carter stands next to him. Carter is holding his crime scene photos up next to the book while he compares them against the pictures inside. His forehead wrinkles while he studies their similarities. Rakim is nodding and whispering something that I can't make out.

And then he notices me. Rakim smiles and gestures with his hand as he calls out, "I'll be with you in moment." He squints as if he recognizes me, but his eyes strain in the low light. I smile and nod with my head held low before rounding the corner near the register. Then I venture into the second half of the store.

This half isn't much different than the other. I've been here before. Many times, in fact. I don't bother with the pretense of looking around. I know what I'm here for.

I walk briskly past the small shelves and items on display, heading toward the back of the store. *There you are*—my ancient tomahawk. A little card in front of the exhibit reads, "Blood of the Cherokee." The yellow overhead light shines upon the weapon as it rests on a stone display. A writing posted on the wall states, "DO NOT TOUCH," in large letters. A taxidermized hawk sits on a pedestal next to the weapon; it glares at me with focused black eyes.

The hatchet's blade is made of sharpened bone; the front is broad, and the back comes to a sharp point. It's affixed to a wooden handle, and black feathers hang from tassels along the side. I glance over my shoulder before taking it in my hands. I stare down at it greedily, running the sharpened bone against my fingers, feeling its cutting tension. *It'll do the work*, I think to myself, smiling and breathing heavily.

Below the display is a history of the item. It tells me what I already know; it's the reason I sought it out. The tool was used in a massacre during the earliest days of the southern colonies. A great conquest in which it butchered the innocent without mercy. It was a cold, vengeful bloodletting; a way of settling the score for a wrong committed. It's one of the few relics that survived to tell the story. And now, it shall tell *mine*.

With the hatchet now in hand, I begin walking back toward the other half of the store. I test its weight as I come to the edge of the doorway that divides the room. I stop at a display just before the opening and watch them. They're still talking among themselves while Rakim leans down to search the shelves for another volume. He pulls it off the shelf and begins flipping through it alongside the detective. Carter feigns interest at first, but he loses focus once he notices a preserved animal fetus that's floating in a jar of murky fluid.

I advance cautiously. I do not wish to be observed wielding my new-found toy, so I hold it by my side as I cross through the opening. I walk in a light, brisk manner toward the shelves. My feet glide over the floor; I am entirely unnoticed. Rakim doesn't even bother to look up from the pages of the book that he's skimming. Carter is holding the fetus jar with both hands now, staring with disgust at the contents inside. I can hear him mumbling something as I approach the corner of the aisle.

I take a deep breath and feel the calm wash over me. I let it last only a moment; for I am now stepping toward the center of the aisle with the hatchet hanging loosely by my side. A subtle grin spreads across my face as I stare at them with my head held low.

"Sir!" Rakim chastises me. He shakes his head and begins walking toward me. "Please do not touch that! Hand it to me, and I'll put it back where it belongs."

I don't say anything; I just stare. I can see his impatience growing as he continues toward me with his arm outstretched. Carter glares at me with a question forming on his lips. His eyes cut into me, and I can tell that he recognizes the figure standing before him.

As Rakim approaches, I raise the hatchet to the right of my head and swing it deftly toward him. The blow lands on his left shoulder; the bone cuts deeply into his flesh. It's stuck there as the man glares at me in disbelief. The reality of it doesn't set in for a couple of seconds. Rakim lowers his trembling head and sees that the weapon is stuck firmly into his shoulder. Blood pours from the wound and soaks his sleeve. His deltoid is nearly cut in half; the gore is palpable and entrancing.

By now, Carter has snapped out of his uncertain delirium. The shock of seeing me has worn off, and he's drawing his service weapon. I position my body just behind Rakim's, using the shop owner as a shield while he cries out in pain. Blood flows from his shoulder once I remove the hatchet. Carter fires as I continue wrestling with the man. The bullet catches me in my right bicep while I struggle against Rakim.

I cry out, but the shot does not slow me down. I've got Rakim directly in front of me now, with my arm wrapped tight around his neck. He's not putting up much of a fight. I lock eyes with Carter, and I know that he dares not shoot me with this innocent man in the way. We stare at each other for a few seconds longer, sizing one another up. His eyes are cold and calculating. I can see that his finger is itching for release; he's merely waiting for his moment to pounce.

I shove Rakim toward him hard. He stumbles and nearly loses his balance. Carter is about five or six feet away, but my overwhelming force sends the pair of them colliding. Rakim falls to his knees and then cowers against the shelf while he clutches his wound. His head hangs low as he winces, gasping for breath.

Carter regains his balance and raises the pistol toward me. But I set upon him too quickly. I grab his outstretched arm as he squeezes the trigger. His shot misses, and it shatters a jar across the room. Carter struggles against me and begins punching me in the jaw with his free hand.

I shake off his blows while I keep a tight hold of his arm. Carter presses against me with all his strength; the seasoned detective is sturdy for an older man. He's doing his best to aim the barrel at me as we wrestle against one another.

I raise the hatchet to my side, but Carter uses his free arm to catch my blow. We're locked against each other now in a test of wills. But my advantage is depravity, and mine knows no bounds. I shove him hard against the shelf and then try pressing the hatchet into his face. Carter's dazed by the impact, but it's not enough to break his hold. He continues struggling against me as we reach another stalemate.

My eyes glow a pale blue while he stares at me in shock. Carter can't believe what he's seeing. I am folklore, legend, an unrivaled force that he cannot contend with. Newfound strength surges within my veins. I begin twisting his right wrist until it breaks in my hand. I can hear the bones cracking as he cries out; his shoulder slumps as the pain courses through his body.

Carter is brought low as I maintain my grasp on his broken wrist. He releases my arm as he leans against the shelf. I jerk him back up by the wrist. His face is bitter and contorted as he screams in agony.

I raise my hatchet as I glare at the effete vermin cowering before me. His softness is revolting; his vulnerability enrages me. I twist his arm while tightening my grasp. Carter's fingers desperately clutch onto the pistol, but it appears to be slipping from his grasp. I swing the hatchet and it slices neatly through his forearm. The hand falls to the ground, still clutching its weapon dutifully.

Then I release the detective; his body drops to the floor like dead weight. Carter's on his knees, propping himself up with his remaining hand. He's howling as he stares down at his arm in disbelief. His eyes flit between his wound and the severed portion lying on the ground nearby.

Then I place my boot on Carter's back as I glare at him derisively. I feast on the injured man's nakedness, but I cannot feed my hunger for long, because a hard blow lands upon my back. It cuts into me and sends me jolting forward. The hatchet slips from my grasp as I fall against the shelf; it teeters for a second before toppling over with a loud thud. I reach behind me and feel it—a ceremonial dagger is wedged between my shoulder blades.

Rakim is staring at me now. He's not sure what to do. His idiotic mouth hangs open as I turn around and stare at him. I begin drawing the blade from my back with my right hand. It's an awkward angle; it takes some maneuvering, but the man stays frozen in place as I pull it out. Rakim stares incredulously for a second longer before he starts glancing around the shop for another weapon.

I draw the dagger out and then hold it down by my right side, studying its ornate markings under the dim light. I smile as the man lunges toward the display again. He picks up a glass jar and throws it at me. I move out of the way as he's fetching another. And another. I'm taking my time, moving toward him slowly. Rakim finally connects with one of the jars, and now I've had enough, so I charge forward and tackle him to the ground.

Rakim starts begging and crying like the miserable wretch that he is. I'm on top of him now. He won't look at me. His eyes are shut while his head shakes back and forth. But after several seconds, the man settles down and begins to weep.

As I raise the dagger overhead, Rakim finally opens his eyes. He's startled and struggles to break free. All his maneuvering forces me to miss the mark as I lower the blade upon him. It slices off half his ear as he strains beneath me.

Rakim's bloody chunk of flesh remains stuck on the tip of my blade as I raise it up again. I quickly begin stabbing him in the shoulders and upper arms. The man cries out with each thrust. He's becoming weaker after being pierced several times. I raise the knife far overhead and then drive it deeply into his chest. A wheezing gasp chokes from his sagging lips.

Then I hear footsteps staggering behind me. As I glance over my shoulder, I see Carter hobbling toward me as quickly as he can. He practically falls over on top of me, grasping with his remaining hand. I elbow him hard in the gut, knocking the wind out of him. Carter falls on his ass, then leans against a shelf; the man is dizzy and gasping for air as I refocus my attention on the shop owner.

I glare at Rakim with animal hatred coursing through me. My body shakes as I press the blade into his sternum and force my weight on top of it. I stare into his dying eyes as he takes his final breath. I'm still straddling his waist, but I draw myself back, breathing deeply and recovering from my efforts. After several seconds, I glance over at the small shelf and notice that the detective has gone.

Then I turn my head and see Carter staggering toward the rows of bookshelves. *There you are*, I think to myself. His head shakes lightly as he struggles to maintain focus. I put my hand to the ground and then push myself up to my feet. He's grabbing the gun from his severed hand, prying it from the cold grip of his lifeless fingers.

Carter is wobbly on his feet as he stands back up. I can tell that gun feels heavy in his weak hand. I'm not overly concerned here. I take my time walking toward him. I calmly wait for him to turn around while holding the dagger down by my leg.

Carter turns and glares at me through a pair of bleary eyes. His lips are parted as he begins sluggishly raising the pistol with his left hand. I can tell that he's fading. His head bobs while his vision betrays him. I smile as I move quickly out of sight. He fires the pistol, but he's too late and misses me entirely.

Then I run down the aisle next to his, keeping low while he scans for me. As I reach the end, I spot a light switch on the wall. I grin to myself as I switch them off. It's quite dark inside now; the only light coming in is from the thin rays creeping in from the single window.

Carter is at the end of his aisle now. He's breathing so loudly that I can hear it from the opposite side of the shelf. I take cover along the edge and listen for his movements. He's leaning on the corner of the shelf; his bleeding arm is held close to his chest, and he's starting to peek around to the other side.

The detective looks down the neighboring aisle and sees that I'm not there. I move silently down the adjacent row while he continues searching. Carter staggers out into the open store and then spots me as I approach. The struggling man stumbles, raising his pistol again. He fires off another negligent shot, and the bullet flies into the ceiling.

Carter is doing his best to aim at me with his left hand as I close the final distance. His hand is outstretched and shaking as I grab hold of it. I wrench his arm. The man cries out but maintains a loose grip on the pistol. He looks up at me with defiance. "You miserable son of a bitch..." he grouses, panting and grimacing while he shakes his head.

I stab him in the neck. It takes some effort, but I'm able to push the blade until it runs clear through. I release his arm, and he staggers away with a few aimless steps. Carter's eyes begin glossing over as strength flees his body. He tries raising his pistol to fire again, but his arm moves so slowly that I'm able to push his hand away with gentle ease. Then I take the gun from him.

As Carter falls to his knees, I look down at the bleeding man with a false, empathetic smile. I shake my head as the gun hangs by the trigger guard from one finger. I sigh with pleasure, tossing the pistol across the store; it clatters on the ground in the opening to the second half.

Blood spurts from the detective's wound; it slows to a gush as I stare into his eyes. The room falls entirely silent except for the wet sucking sounds that he makes while clutching his throat. Carter's eyes grow wide and panicked as he begins to suffocate.

I place my hand on the blade's handle. "The path of righteousness has betrayed you, Detective," I tell him calmly. Then I move my hand to his forehead while he takes short, shallow breaths; his head quivers as he looks to the floor. I push him to the side, and his body falls upon the nearby shelf. It teeters for a moment before settling; several items fall to the floor and land on the ground near him.

I squat down next to him; our faces are only a few feet apart now. Carter is on the verge of death as he slumps against the bookcase. The man's unable to lift his head any longer. He's pathetic and frail—a creature of my subjugation.

I grab a fistful of hair and take hold of Carter's head. Its weight is completely unsupported. I turn it to and fro, smiling at him like a child who's cherishing their favorite toy. I grunt with satisfaction while releasing him from my grasp. His head sags to his shoulder as drool forms on his lips.

Then I glance over and spot the hatchet that's still lying on the floor. I grin as I reach out and grab it. I take Carter by his head again and then raise the hatchet overhead. He's barely clinging to life as I lower it swiftly; the blade enters high on his cheek and practically severs half his jaw. It slices all the way through to his lips. There's no reaction. There's nothing left. I've taken all that he had to give.

The hatchet is still stuck inside Carter's face as I release the handle. I stand up and allow him to fall to the floor. He's a pitiful sight, lying there on his side with the dagger protruding through his neck and the hatchet dug into his face. Blood pools around his body. I nudge him with my foot and smile as I watch all that red flow onto the floor.

V.

Raven and the Fairy Metaphysical Shop
February 3, 2025
12:55 p.m.

"Yes, Your Honor, I understand," Amara replies. She's holding the phone to her ear after crossing the street. "They're sending more officers to your chambers. We'll also put a patrol car outside your home until everything is resolved." Amara pauses on the sidewalk as she gets an earful of his frightened demands.

They continue talking for another few minutes before Amara heads toward their parked Crown Victoria. After they hang up, she places the phone back into her pocket, opens the passenger door, and reaches inside. She leans against the armrest while searching the backseat. "There you are," she mutters, feeling the thin wooden cross lying on the floorboards.

Amara is sitting in the passenger seat and looking down at the cross when she hears something loud pop across the street. She glances back over toward the building. Several seconds pass and then another muffled pop rings out. Concern spreads across her face as she gets out of the car quickly. She closes the door, puts the cross inside her jacket pocket, and draws her pistol. Amara starts walking briskly across the street as she stares at the building suspiciously. A third pop rings out, and this time, there's no mistaking the sound. It's gunfire, and she knows it.

Pedestrians begin hurrying away from the storefronts when they hear the shots ring out. Amara closes the remaining distance with her pistol at the ready. She glances inside the small window near the door, but she's unable to see anything inside. Amara cracks the door open cautiously, scanning the room before she enters. Then she pushes it open and raises her pistol as she steps inside.

"Carter!" she calls out. Her fretful eyes dart across the room. Eerie silence fills the shop while she waits for a response that will not come. Amara aims the pistol to her right and glances into the second half of the store. Seeing no one, she turns her head to the left.

Amara stares in wonder when she spots Rakim sprawled upon the floor. His haunting, frozen eyes stare back into hers while she advances toward him. Amara steps cautiously to avoid the pool of blood beneath his body. She cuts her eyes with nervous tension, taking in all that surrounds her. And as she turns, she spots her friend lying mangled on the ground.

Amara rushes toward him. She crouches next to Carter and stares at him in shock, but she doesn't bother checking for a pulse. His empty eyes and the blade running through his neck tell her everything she needs to know.

The detective glances around and checks her surroundings before pulling out her cellphone. She places a call. As Amara puts the phone to her ear, she catches something out of the corner of her eye. A shadow passes by at the end of the row. She puts the phone in her pocket and stands up quickly while she raises her gun. "Atlanta PD!" she shouts. "Come out with your hands on top of your head."

She's convincing, I must say. Her authoritative tone masks her fear quite well, but the pistol trembles in her hand as she steps slowly down the aisle. The overcast sky dims the thin sunlight creeping in through the window. Amara listens intently as she advances through the darkened room.

I see her barrel popping out from the end of her aisle, and it's time to make my departure. I rip the curtain open and then raise the window. My leg is hanging halfway out when I hear her call out behind me, "Stop or I'll shoot!"

I smile at her as the outside light shines upon my face. She gets a good glimpse of me and seems utterly confounded. *How can it be?* her eyes say to mine. I admire her warmly while she stares at me with burning intensity. I raise a hand to my lips and blow her a kiss as I allow myself to fall from the window.

She hesitates for a moment and then rushes toward the windowsill. Her hungry eyes scour the scene below. The alley is vacant. She looks right and sees that it's sealed off by the adjoining buildings. The sound of the blowing wind caresses her ear. She hops out of the window, runs down the alley, and then stops near the street.

Amara is nearly frantic as she stands on the sidewalk, searching. A few pedestrians move around her while she remains puzzled by the roadside. I am nowhere to be found. And I know what she must be thinking: *was he ever really here?*

But I am ghost. I am phantom, and I'm every malignant wish ever brought true. And soon, my darling, we shall be together in all the blackest ways possible.

Chapter Ten

I.

Detective Cruz's Apartment

February 5, 2025

7:30 p.m.

Amara's one-bedroom apartment is a scattered mess. She sits on her couch with various pictures and folders strewn around her. A glass of red wine sits on her living room table. She's wearing black slacks and a white blouse while she sorts through the evidence surrounding her. Her energy is stretched and muddled as she flips through the documents and photos. She's worked herself onto the verge of collapse since finding Carter dead inside the metaphysical shop.

Amara places a thin pile of crime scene photos on the table and sighs. The long hours she's been putting in are beginning to take their toll. She raises her fingertips to the bridge of her nose and starts rubbing her eyes.

Then Amara raises her head and allows her eyes to drift across the room. They move without purpose before settling upon her dining room table. She glares at the glass and takes her time before reaching a decision, then she stands up and walks toward it.

Amara hovers over the table, studying the book she'd taken from the crime scene earlier. She stares at the letters on the cover. "The Serpent's Call: An Introduction to Black Magic," it reads. The words practically form on her lips. Cynthia's wooden cross is laid to the side of it.

Amara's mouth moves to one side as she reaches down to pick up the book. She stares at its cover for several seconds longer. Then she begins walking away before looking back and retrieving the cross. She starts thumbing through the book slowly as she makes her way to the couch.

After Amara takes her seat, she continues examining the pages. The first section details snake worship across various cultures. As Amara skims the words, she develops a greater understanding. The mythos is displayed in numerous drawings and sketches of ancient peoples gathered in awe before mighty serpents. They worship them as deities.

Amara is near the end of the book when she stops flipping through it. She places her finger beneath a chapter heading that reads, "Countering Black Magic." Underneath the chapter heading is a vivid depiction of the Fall of Man. Eve lies dejected and nude near a tranquil stream in the forest. Adam sits next to her, reaching his arm toward her in existential angst. Two black birds glide gently in the background. A foreboding canopy of dense foliage hangs above them; a serpent slithers into the distance as they enter a new world together.

Beneath the picture is a smaller section entitled, "Banishing Evil Entities." It lists a simple spell below: "Behold, I shall be not afraid, but trust in the stars of Heaven; its righteous constellations give thee no light, and the sun will starve thy malice. At eventide, trouble, but before morning, ruin."

There's a recipe listed beneath the spell. It suggests collecting dirt from the shoes of your enemy, then mixing it with cayenne pepper, sassafras, and coffee grounds. "For best results," it says, "sprinkle the mixture in front of your enemy's door to force him from your community." Underneath the spell, there's a sentence written in bold: "Your adversary's presence will vex you no longer; he will rot and perish from your world."

Amara reads through the book pensively while clutching the crucifix. She begins digesting it all. Her eyes drift toward the coffee table again as her anxious, disordered mind starts to wander. The crime scene photographs of Carter and Rakim seem to call to her; she fixes her eyes upon them.

Amara picks up the stack of photographs. She sorts through them one by one, examining each picture with careful attention. After seeing several photos of her partner in a row, she stops, sighs, and her overtired expression gives way to gloom.

Amara resumes studying the photos after a moment's break. She's reaching the end of the set when she comes to a picture of Judge Erickson. Something strikes her as she stares into the picture, perplexed. Amara reflects on it for several seconds and then stands up with renewed purpose.

It's like she's caught a second wind as she hurries toward the dining room table. Amara tosses the stack of photos onto the glass. She grabs her keys, her gun, and her badge, then throws on her jacket as she makes her way out of the apartment.

II.

Outside of Fulton County Superior Court
February 5, 2025
7:30 p.m.

I can't stop thinking of her. My thoughts plague me night and day; they're vile and invasive. I think of her flowing dark hair, the shape of her body as she glides. Something in me longs for something in her, but I cannot place my finger upon it. She taunts me, torments me, and now I must do the same to her.

I shake my head with vigor to rid myself of the oppression. Then I slap myself in the face, and the mark that it leaves pushes me toward my task. As always, there remains work to be done. I must stay sharp.

The twilight sky continues darkening around me as I pace the sidewalk. The chilly air laps at my neck. I walk briskly along the path and raise the collar on a long black coat that I found. My frozen eyes burn holes into the pavement while I focus on what lies ahead. My breath comes like the beating of drums; they pound for endless war.

I pass beneath a streetlamp and then pause once I reach the shadows. I lean against a tall oak tree on the lawn that leads up to the courthouse, scanning the scene around me. There are two cops out front. Most have gone home by now. Only a few scattered windows are still lit up at this hour. But...given the attention my recent activities have received, I'm sure that the judge feels safer here, more at home. But home can be a dangerous place too; I assure you, old man.

The two officers are standing atop a long set of stone stairs leading to the courthouse entrance. Tall pillars surround them on either side as they sip coffee and joke with one another. The gray sky above paints the building a dark, faded blue. The façade near the entrance is white stone; dark brick encases it on either side. The structure is covered in an eerie shadow that calls out to me; it welcomes my advance.

I move to the right. I don't wish for the police up top to spot me, so I maintain a good distance from them as I start searching for a way inside. A black iron gate surrounds the exterior of the building. I'm lurking around the fence about two hundred feet away from the entrance when I see a police sketch posted on a streetlight. I tear it down and examine it. It's me, all right. They did a fairly good job, I must say. I smirk as I ball the paper up and toss it on the ground.

Here's a place that's as good as any, I think to myself. The streets around me are strangely deserted. There are little spikes placed atop the ends of the fence, but that won't stop me. I take a final glance around as I begin hoisting myself up. Once I reach the top, the spikes dig into my flesh. They tear my shirt while I shift myself onto the other side. It draws a little blood, but that's to be expected. I touch the wound and see that it's nothing serious.

There's a long row of windows along the first floor. I gaze inside the closest one. The lights are off, but as I peer inside, I can see that it's a conference room. The coast is still clear. I reach into my waistband and draw a crowbar. I begin working it against the window's ledge. It's tearing into the wood as I exert myself against it. The window pops open as the small metal lock inside gives way.

I open the window the rest of the way, tuck the crowbar back inside my jacket, and then crawl inside. I look around the darkened room. Scant light creeps in from the window on the door. There're a few rows of gray tables and a white board at the front of the room. I walk quietly toward the door and peer out, moving my head from side to side to get a better angle.

I hear footsteps making their way across the dirty gray floor. A middle-aged cop with oily black hair passes by the window, and for a second, I almost think he spots me. I lean into the shadows and watch him pass by the door as an idea flashes through my mind.

I creak the door open as gently as I possibly can. Then I peek out and see that there is no one else in the long, open hallway. I draw a small weapon from my jacket pocket; it's a pair of brass knuckles with a three-inch blade on the end. I slink out of the doorway and begin sneaking behind him. It feels as though my feet aren't even touching the ground as I slide toward the man without effort.

I'm mere feet away now, close enough to reach out and touch him. Carefully, I make my move. I place my left hand over his mouth and pull him toward me. He's taken aback by the sudden jolt and nearly loses his balance. I begin punching him several times in the spine, driving the blade in and out as quickly as possible.

He starts biting my fingers. I gnash my teeth to avoid crying out. Then I start pulling him back toward the door while he struggles against me. Tremendous strength flows through my veins as I usher him inside. His legs kick and flail, but I hold him steady in my grasp.

I'm still stabbing him over and over as we clear the doorway. His yelps and cries are muted beneath my fingers. I can feel the back of his shirt starting to grow wet; his blood drips onto my boots and the floor below. My feet make a terrible mess of things; I'm leaving bloody footprints on the carpet as we walk together.

My hand is drenched in his warmth when I throw his body onto the floor. He's gasping and trying to crawl away on his hands and knees. The man starts reaching for his gun, but I mount myself on top of him, pushing him down again. He struggles against me, pushing up with his hips. He's doing his best to throw me off, but I will not budge.

As he continues thrashing, I jam the blade into the side of his neck, dragging it across with great effort. The veins in my forehead bulge as I slice cleanly through his wet tissue. I push his face into the floor and let him bleed out for a few seconds. His struggle subsides, and I feel his gentle spasms working themselves out beneath me.

The man finally stops moving. I sigh with relief, enjoying my moment of pure completion. "*What a rush,*" I whisper in a self-congratulating tone. I wipe the bloody weapon on my jacket and then place it back inside my pocket. I look down at my ruined clothes and then back at the dead officer while I begin nurturing an idea.

"Hmm..." I start nodding my head as the thought grows on me. "It could be fun," I say, raising myself from the floor. I begin taking off my all-black clothes in the darkened room and start setting them in a pile on the ground.

I am down to my socks and underwear when I begin undressing the dead cop. I remove his boots first. Then I take off his dark blue pants, belt, shirt, and hat. I put them all on and smile as I gaze down at myself with my hands on my hips. I'm wedging my thumbs underneath the duty belt like they like to do. I'm an upstanding citizen—*just like the rest of you*. I'm beaming with pride at the thought of it.

Well, there's no use in wasting time. I should get a move on. I walk back to the door and peer out again. All is still quiet. It's not until I open the door and the hall light shines upon me that I realize that I'm still covered in blood. Thankfully, his dark blue uniform masks it all rather well. I can only hope that it won't immediately draw everyone's attention. Either way, it'll have to do. I wipe my bloody arms and hands on the dark pants, spitting on them as necessary to wipe the gore clean.

At this hour, I can't just walk around the courthouse in an unconvincing manner. I think back to the wanted poster—they're on the lookout for me, so I push my long dark hair into the hat to conceal it. What a *handsome* officer I am. I smile at my reflection as I pass by a door near the stairwell.

I'm on the first floor of the courthouse. It's almost a basement, really. I come to a half-turn staircase, glance up, and listen for any movement. There's no one down here, but on the main floor upstairs, I can hear several sets of footsteps and hushed voices. I begin making my way up the flight cautiously with my eyes fixed above.

I make it to the second floor and then take stock of the area. There's a cop walking down the hallway about thirty feet away. A receptionist sits behind the front desk near the large wooden doors. She stares absently at her computer screen.

I notice that there's a directory hanging on the wall near the staircase. I smile to myself as I peruse its contents. "Erickson...Judge Erickson," I say, guiding my finger down the list. I stop when I reach his name and see that he's on the third floor. Room 333.

The receptionist gazes at me curiously. I smile and tilt my hat before heading back toward the stairwell. She's arching her eyebrow as I walk away. I make my way up the stairs again. As I'm heading up, another cop is walking down the flight. He's chomping on a piece of gum and staring at me. Come on, *come on*, don't notice me, I'm thinking.

The gawking idiot furrows his bushy eyebrows, but I keep my head down to avoid his gaze. I can tell that he's wondering who I am and why he doesn't recognize me. Can he see the stains on my uniform? It doesn't matter—I must keep moving and cannot be detained. I hold my breath as we pass one another and then breathe a sigh of relief as I make it to the next landing without incident.

The third floor seems more formal than the second. I look around and everything seems antiquated. All the wood appears to be polished; it gives off an archaic shine. The walls are decorated with portraits of esteemed judges who have long since passed. I head down the hallway toward the offices. The lights in the hall are dim; there are bookshelves filled with matching red volumes of legal texts along the walls. I gaze into a few empty courtrooms as I pass by.

I can *feel* his presence nearby. I can smell him. I know that he's close...he's working late in his chambers, like the good civil servant that he is. His tireless clerks are there too, fetching some document that he needs or bringing legal arguments for him to review. Yes, the old, gray judge is safe behind his little door...and probably signing off on someone's fate right now. I'm sure of it.

III.

Inside Fulton County Superior Court

February 5, 2025

7:50 p.m.

I'm rounding a corner as the numbers on the doors grow closer and closer to Judge Erickson's chambers. I'm about to turn left when I catch myself and spot two uniformed cops on guard. They're not paying close attention. They're both sitting on a bench, looking down at their phones, but I can't exactly go waltzing past them. I press my body against the corner and glance across the hall at the room number. It's 332. That means the door these two swine are posted in front of must be the judge's chambers. I must get rid of them.

I sigh as I begin thinking of what to do next. I go fully behind the corner and lean against the wall. An idea hits me as my eyes settle across the hall. I spot an emergency exit leading to a stairwell. A subtle smirk forms on my lips as I check over my shoulder and begin walking toward the door.

Then I open the emergency exit and step inside the stairwell. I peek my head out while keeping the door propped open with my foot. Hmm...what would work best? I'm reflecting on the question as I glance down at my duty belt. I don't want to raise too much alarm, but some of these things could prove useful. Ah, *yes*...now I've got it.

I remove the flashlight from my belt. It's a long and sturdy device. I click it on and off a few times for good measure. Then I lean out into the hallway with the light switched on. I hear the grumpy, middle-aged cop on the left tell his younger partner that he's going to go take a piss. "Hold down the fort," he tells him. The younger man nods and smiles while his rotund counterpart walks down the hallway toward the bathrooms.

Once the older cop is out of view, I roll the flashlight onto the ground. It travels several feet before stopping in the center of the hallway. The lights inside the hall are just dim enough for the flashlight beam to carry. The moving light catches the officer's attention from the corner of his eye. He turns his head and examines it with curiosity. He's squinting down the hall while moving his lips to one side. Something's not right, he must be thinking. And like a good boy, he gets up to investigate.

The young blonde officer paces slowly down the hall with one hand in his pocket. He cranes his neck to try to see around the corner. He moves a little to the right as he rounds the corner suspiciously. There's nothing, no one. His eyes dart around the empty hallway as a puzzled look spreads across his face. He bends down and picks up the flashlight. The man studies it and sees that it's the same as his—police issued.

The officer pauses for a moment as though he's waiting for something to happen. He shifts his gaze to the emergency exit and notices that it's propped open. He stares at it uncertainly for a moment before the lights start flickering on and off inside. This happens three times before they are turned off again.

The man undoes the button on his holster, resting his hand atop the pistol grip. He draws his flashlight and enters the stairwell. Then he clicks his light on and scans the wall for a switch. After he finds it, he flips it several times, but it does nothing. Still in darkness, the man grows frustrated while he shines his light around the landing.

The officer points his light up the stairwell leading to the fourth floor. I lean back into the shadows. I'm watching him beneath me; he's moving his light around and straining his neck to see. I draw my large bowie knife just in case he decides to come up and investigate.

The officer stands there for a moment, hoping the darkness will call out and reveal itself to him. It doesn't. My black eyes follow him from the shadows as he walks toward the staircase leading to the second floor below.

I start creeping down the staircase without making the faintest sound. I am a silent stream of water, moving through everything with ease. The officer seems disappointed when he sees nothing below. He takes a step down the flight and shines his light down the hole, finding nothing but the partial rows of stairs beneath him. There's no life, no movement.

He's just starting to turn around when I take him in my grasp. I grab the man by the collar and stab him in the neck. The blade slices through his flesh as blood spurts onto the stairwell. It fires off in torrents as he clutches his neck; he's wheezing and struggling to keep his balance against the guardrail. The gushing officer goes for his gun with his free hand, but I intervene. I stop him by stabbing him in the gut several times.

Then I drive the knife into his belly while pulling him toward me with my other hand. I press the blade in firmly as I take the pistol from his grasp. Then I drop his gun down the hole in the stairwell. It clatters loudly after falling three stories. The man stares at me through fading, spellbound eyes. I smirk and grunt as I toss him carelessly down the stairs.

The officer's body twists and rolls down the flight. He stops at the bottom of the landing beneath a dim fluorescent emergency light. It shines upon his face. He's bunched up against the wall at the bottom, staring up at me.

I study the man while he struggles to breathe. His head is pressed against the wall, and his chin sags to his chest. The dying officer is trying to move, but he can't summon the strength. I stare down at him for a few seconds longer, watching him wilt and wane. I don't need to finish him off. He'll be dead in minutes, and I'd prefer him to suffer for a while, anyway.

I leave him there to rot and die. I tuck the knife back into my belt, open the door, and then peek my head out. No one's coming, so I creep back to the same corner as before. My second friend is back, and he's stuffing a snack he got from the vending machine down his fat gullet. He stares at his phone absently as he settles back onto the bench.

I emerge from the corner and then start walking briskly toward him. My eyes are sharpened with great purpose. He doesn't see me advancing—he's just sitting there, eating, and scrolling with no idea of what's to come. "This lazy motherfucker...just going to leave his post," he complains, shaking his head as he continues chewing. His eyes grow wide as he becomes entranced by a football game on his phone.

I stop just a few paces away from him and stand there, waiting for him to notice me. He doesn't look up. "Where'd you go?" the man asks in a lazy, sarcastic tone. When he doesn't get an answer within a few seconds, he turns his head toward me.

The officer appears startled when he glances up and sees that I'm not his partner. He straightens himself up, placing the snack and his phone on the bench next to him. "Who, uh, who are you?" he questions, looking me up and down. I can see his body tensing up; I can feel his uncertainty.

The man can probably see the blood on my uniform. He doesn't want to alert me, but he's guiding his hand toward his weapon just in case. I can see more questions beginning to form on his lips when I answer him, "I'm death."

I quickly draw the service weapon from my duty belt and shoot him in the neck. He slumps against the bench upon impact. His eyes grow bloodshot while his face turns red. Blood shoots from the wound at first and then slows to a gush. And before he gets the bright idea of killing me before he dies, I shoot him in the head. He's dead instantaneously. His eyes grow hollow, and the body becomes empty flesh.

There's no time to linger here. My eyes shift immediately to the door of room 333. A little inscription beneath the room number reads, "Judge Erickson's Chambers." It's always nice to know you're in the right place. I open the door and step inside.

One of the judge's clerks is standing from his chair in a panic. He's in his mid-thirties with blonde hair and rolled sleeves. The man gapes at me as I enter. He's frozen in place with his hands on his desk.

"Hello!" I greet him with a wide smile and bulging eyes. I shoot him in the forehead, and he falls back against the wall. There's a desk facing his just a few feet away. A woman with dark hair, a black blazer, and matching skirt shrieks when she sees her colleague being stricken down.

The woman rushes to the floor and starts cowering at the foot of her desk. She's trying to crawl under it—as if that will do anything to save her. I step toward her and shoot her three times in the back. The impact forces her to collapse. I leave her there to take her last few breaths, then walk toward the door in the center of the room and open it.

Judge Erickson is staring at me with a pair of frightened marshmallow eyes. He's wearing his black robe, but he seems infinitely smaller than he did in that courtroom. I close the door calmly behind me. Then I cut my eyes toward him in a slow, sinister manner as I return the pistol to my holster.

The judge lurches from behind his desk, but I block his path. He pauses there, staring at me. It's sinking in for him, I can see it. His wide, hanging mouth says it all: *he's back from the grave, the madness was true.*

The man of esteemed reason struggles to keep his wits; it's almost too much for him to process. Judge Erickson raises his hands defensively. He starts trudging through some vain, helpless plea before I interrupt him. I seize him by the wrists, and all his ineffectual begging comes to a screeching halt. "No, no, it's time to die, old man," I tell him in a heightened, manic voice. I grind my teeth as I stare into his soul with great malice. He lets out some pitiful noise—something between a groan and a broken, powerless cry.

I can't help but laugh as he tries freeing himself from my grip. My hands are iron shackles wrapped tightly around his wrists. My glaring eyes convey a simple message to his: you will never escape this. I release one of his hands as I reach down and draw the pistol. He tries to pull away again, but I still have a tight hold on his other arm.

Judge Erickson winces and looks back at me. He raises his free hand to protect himself once he sees me raising the gun. I thump him hard on the head with the bottom of the pistol grip. He reels from the pain and keeps his hand close to his forehead. Blood starts trickling from the wound as he begins to weep. *The poor, pitiful scum.*

He stops pulling and just stares at the floor dejectedly. There's a good boy. Accept your fate...accept what I give you. I set the pistol down on his desk and punch him hard on the temple. He cries out and then falls to his knees with me still clutching onto his limp wrist.

I draw the knife from my belt and hold it loosely in my hand while Judge Erickson cowers beneath me. He's pleading and crying. "Don't do it," he implores. I drag his wrist toward me and then slice it vertically. It leaves a long red stream that begins growing and spilling.

I lick the tip of the blade as he shrinks beneath me. He's trying to curl into the fetal position. It's a rather bizarre sight. I'm still holding onto him as he lowers himself to the ground in utter degradation. I want to take it all from him, *everything*. I want his establishment, his prestige burned to the ground so that I can defile the ashes.

I jerk him back toward me and then punch him in the face again. His head starts to slump, so I dig a thumb in his eye. I exert pressure while he cries out in pain. As I release my thumb, I can see that his other eye is still searching around frantically.

He makes a feeble attempt to reach for the pistol on the table. As he does, I lower the blade swiftly and chop off the tips from two of his fingers. He screams and glares at his hand as he falls back to his knees. I finally release him. Then I push his head against the desk, pick up the pistol, and press it against the back of his head.

The judge starts sobbing more and more; he's begging me to just do it already. *Not yet*, I'm thinking. A malicious smile spreads across my face, but then I hear something—loud shouting and hurried footsteps are coming toward me. I pull the judge onto his feet as I hear the outside door opening. Then I wrap my left arm around the man's throat as I press the gun against his temple. I turn us both around, stare at the door, and wait for them to enter.

I see them turning the handle cautiously. Then, in a single violent motion, two cops barge in. They're aiming their guns and shouting their orders, but I remain steadfast. I will not be shaken. Refusing to acknowledge them, I simply stare. They will not shoot for fear of hitting the judge. I peek my eyes out from behind his head while his body shields me.

The judge is mumbling to himself and bleeding all over me, so I tighten my hold around his neck; he grimaces under the pressure. The blood from his forehead begins streaming down his cheeks. My eyes start searching around involuntarily. My position here has become untenable. I'm pulling the judge back a pace or two as I glance behind me—I see a window. It's the only option, really.

As I turn back toward them, my eyes meet the gaze of the young officer. "You'll never make it," he warns.

"Drop your weapon and release Judge Erickson!" the other barks.

My precious black aura has joined us. It creeps into the room and then grows quickly, billowing near the two men standing tensely before me. The once well-lit office has grown quite dark; it's like being inside of a storm. The officers maintain their reserve, though they can't help but observe the strange clouds surrounding them.

The man on the left is calling for backup with his clip-on radio. I begin inching toward the window with the gun still pointed at the judge's head. I glance behind me, peering through the glass, and examining the ground below. *I can make it.* It'll be close, but I'll make it.

I smile vaguely at the two officers. Their glaring eyes burn holes with pervading intensity. I lean in close to the judge's ear while still staring at them. "How does it feel, tyrant?" I ask him in a low whisper. Then I lower the weapon and shoot him in the back.

I toss Erickson aside. The cowardly judge falls to the ground in a pitiful show of bloody groveling. Before the officers can even react, I am already firing upon them. The two men release a barrage of bullets in my direction as well. Walls of them are flying through the air as the room ignites with gunfire.

Judge Erickson is caught in between the flying rounds as he tries to crawl away. The bullets tear into his flesh and contort his body; then he sinks into the ground. He howls for just a second before he's cut short by another penetrating round. He lies dead on the ground now; his expression becomes vacant as the blood pools beneath him.

The officers have shot me several times; a few hit my chest and shoulders, and another dug its way deep into my belly. The rest of their shots have simply made a mess of the office—shattering glass, destroying wood, and ripping holes in the judge's belongings. The pain radiates throughout my body, but the dark aura empowers me in ways I've not yet imagined.

I've caught one of them in the leg. The man falls to the ground but continues shooting at me from a kneeling position. I hit the other in his left arm, but he soldiers through the pain. My other shots have missed or hit their bulletproof vests. My gun clicks, and it seems as though our little show is over. Not quite steady on my feet yet, I toss my weapon aside.

While the pair of officers are reloading, I rush toward them. I draw the bowie knife from my belt and stab the kneeling man in the neck. The other takes aim with his pistol, but I manage to stab him in the arm before he can fire another shot. I penetrate him again and again, driving the blade into his gut. The man is quickly subdued once my knife pierces the vest. I shove him off me, and he falls to the ground on his side.

It's time to get out of here. I pick up the chair that's in front of the judge's desk and hurl it through the window. As I'm raising myself onto the window's ledge, I hear more footsteps approaching. I glance behind me and have only enough time to lock eyes with a new officer before he fires on me.

Suddenly, a splitting migraine. Disorientation. The world becomes hazy and unstable as I reel from being shot in the head. As I touch the wounded spot on my skin, I knock my hat to the ground below. My hair is matted and wet with blood. I'm woozy and hemorrhaging. I raise my bloody hand to the window frame to keep my balance, leaving a dense red handprint against the white wall.

The officer is watching me stumble around with his gun still fixed upon me. My knife clatters to the ground, and he makes his move. The man lunges toward me. He takes me in his grasp, and I barely have the residual strength to fight back. He's got a tight grip around my wrists as he tries forcing me against the wall.

We're wrestling against each other right next to the shattered window. I manage to turn around and take hold of his arms. As we push against one another, I lose my balance against the windowsill. I start teetering over the edge, so I grab onto his sleeves tightly.

We're tumbling to the earth below before either of us knows what's happened. We fall onto the sidewalk, and he lands on his back. The man dies upon impact when his head slaps against the pavement. I slowly try to press myself from the ground. My body feels like it weighs a thousand pounds. My arms simply will not perform the work.

As I'm struggling to rise, I glance up and see two officers rushing from the courthouse doors. They're about fifty feet away. A police cruiser barrels down the path toward me with its sirens wailing. I'm unarmed, disabled, but still I persist.

I'm heaving with all my might. My torso begins lifting off the ground as I grunt loudly with exertion. My stringy, bloody hair hangs in my face as I come off the ground. I make it to one knee and start to catch my breath, studying the two men from a distance. They're on the courthouse steps, pointing their guns, and shouting things I couldn't care less about. I clear my throat and spit on the dead man lying next to me.

Then I make it back onto my feet, and the advancing car comes to a screeching halt by the sidewalk in front of the building. Two more pop out of the vehicle and begin shouting with their guns drawn as well. I turn and face them. My hands are curled tightly into fists as I analyze my situation. I weigh all of my options, and none of them seem great.

I don't have it in me to run. I wonder how many more of their bullets I can take. There's only one way to find out. I start walking toward them slowly. The night seems to have taken its toll on me, because I'm limping now with every step.

The men's yelling, the wailing of the sirens, and the sound of a second car approaching all coalesce together. It forms a wall of empty noise while I continue trudging toward them. I hear them call out several more warnings as the second car halts next to the first. I ignore them and keep moving.

I'm only about thirty feet away when I hear the first shot ring out. It strikes the cement by my feet. A second zooms past me. The third strikes me in the chest. The impact jolts me back for a second, but I recover and continue walking toward them.

Suddenly, shots ring out in all directions. All four men and the two behind me all start firing at once. They unload everything that they have. My body is rocking back and forth as I'm being jostled by their bullets. Within a few seconds, I am brought to my knees.

The firing continues. My uniform is pockmarked with bullet holes. I'm drenched in gore, and my body is torn to shreds beneath my clothes. Another shot hits me in the forehead, then I collapse to the pavement.

The sound and the flash of their sirens grow faint. The world starts fading to black once the six shooters stop firing; they watch me dwindle to nothing. After their confusion settles, each swarms upon me with their weapons pointed.

IV.

Outside of Fulton County Superior Court

February 5, 2025

8:20 p.m.

Amara pulls up next to the sidewalk in front of the courthouse. Her eyes grow wide when she spots the flashing lights and cop cars up ahead. She gazes around with a vague sense of alarm while she parks her car. Then she steps out slowly, noticing several uniformed officers placing tape around the scene.

Amara's wearing a white blouse, a black suit, and has her pistol inside a leather sling holster. Several cops are standing around, talking among themselves as she approaches. They exchange empty glances while she flashes her badge and advances toward the body sprawled out on the pavement.

Two cops are standing over the body with their thumbs looped in their belts. Their expressions are blank as they stare down at the corpse. Amara identifies herself. "What happened here?" she asks.

The young, portly officer on the left answers, "We're not really sure yet. Guy just came in and shot several people. Killed Judge Erickson too. He tried to flee the scene, so we fired on him..." He starts shaking his head while raising a hand to his chin. "He just kept staring with dead eyes the whole time."

Amara glances down at the body. Her expression says it all: it's him, all right. Dozens of thoughts begin racing through her mind when the other officer follows up, "We don't have an ID on him yet, though."

"I wouldn't bother," she offers mysteriously.

A few seconds pass as the man studies her with suspicion. Amara looks up and meets his gaze. The officer's radio crackles and a staticky voice comes through the speaker. The man tilts his head as he listens to a voice requesting assistance. He nods and confirms that they're en route. "We'll give you a few minutes here," he tells her. "Not sure whose case this'll be yet."

"Thanks," Amara replies in a flat tone. She hesitates for a moment, watching the pair of them walk toward an officer that's taping off the area. Once they've gotten about twenty feet away, she squats down next to the body. She looks at it with an air of defiance. Amara glances around and sees that no one is nearby. She studies the body for a moment longer and then pulls an evidence bag from her jacket pocket.

"Just in case," she mutters to herself as she grabs hold of the dead man's foot. Amara takes a pen and starts dragging it through the tread of his boots. She carefully collects the dirt into the evidence bag. Then she places the bag back inside her pocket as she stands up again. The weary detective turns around when she hears a car door slamming behind her. She watches as emergency workers unload a gurney from a nearby ambulance.

After half a minute, the workers are wheeling the gurney alongside her. They lower the bed, and then each stands at opposite ends of the body. They hoist it up onto the gurney and raise it again. Amara glares at the corpse, watching them wheel it away toward the ambulance. They load its pallid, unoccupied flesh into their vehicle and then drive away a few minutes later.

Chapter Eleven

I.

Fulton County Morgue

February 5, 2025

10:30 p.m.

The mortician's assistant wheels a covered body on a gurney down a long hallway. The blinding fluorescent lights shine brightly upon the grimy tile floor as the wheels squeak against them. The tired old man looks around nervously as he moves. He wheezes while he pushes the gurney through a pair of swinging double doors.

They close behind him. "Got a John Doe here for you," he informs the mortician. He lets his mouth hang open while he catches his breath. His neck hangs low like a vulture as he scratches his sparse white hair.

The mortician glances over nonchalantly. He's a man in his late fifties, sitting with his legs crossed at his desk. He's wearing thick framed glasses, a lab coat, and a plaid button-up underneath. He wrinkles his bushy eyebrows and runs his fingers through his peppered, unkempt hair. "Thanks, just put him down there on the end," he replies.

The elderly man wheels the gurney over to the last spot in a row of corpses. The bodies are all covered in faded white sheets. Large steel refrigerators surround the area and a variety of chemicals and cutting tools sit in a tray next to them. The weary assistant stares off for a moment before catching himself in a state of inattention. He nods kindly to the mortician after refocusing his mind; then he heads back out the double doors again.

The mortician picks up a sandwich sitting next to him on the desk and takes a bite as he stands from his chair. The bright overhead lights reflect off the metal pans and instruments around him. The sterile white environment gleams and shines, though scattered cockroaches still scurry under the cover of shadows. The mortician studies his notes on a clipboard as he makes his way over to the newest addition.

He makes a final note on the clipboard, then sets it down on the steel countertop next to him. The man stands over the body, lifting the sheet. He glances it over, noticing the obvious multiple gunshot wounds. The dead officer's long, stringy hair is matted in blood; his haunting eyes stare with frozen anger. His shirt had been removed during a failed attempt to resuscitate him once EMS arrived. The man's belongings are collected inside a plastic bag by his feet. The mortician sifts through the bag, examining the officer's tattered uniform with curiosity.

The mortician continues eyeing the dead man, studying his face, and noticing something familiar. He arches his eyebrows while he leans in closer. "It can't be," he mutters with his jaw hanging open. He scans the body up and down. "I know I...wasn't it the same man just a few weeks ago?" He heads back to his desk and starts combing through his files.

When he can't find what he's looking for, he decides to head toward the older records section on the opposite side of the morgue. "I've got to check," he tells himself.

The mortician exits through the swinging doors and heads down the long hallway. Unbeknownst to him, as he enters the records office, a long black snake slithers past him. He heads down the corridor and enters the morgue. The serpent moves intently, gliding across the floor toward the dead officer. He wraps himself around the legs of the gurney, working his way up in a coil. The snake maneuvers onto the corpse. His thick, heavy body rests upon the man's chest.

The serpent is poised. He studies the man through a pair of black, beady eyes while his tongue laps greedily. The snake rises up and towers over him before plunging down and biting his neck. He digs his teeth in deeper as venom begins coursing through the body. The snake releases his hold, then draws back, leaving two thin imprints as black blood begins trickling from the wound.

The room falls silent while the snake hovers over the corpse. The overhead lights grow dim as a pair of clopping hooves creep against the tile floor. They come slowly down the hall and then stop just before the door. It opens with a gentle breeze. Within seconds, a dark apparition appears in the corner of the morgue. The shape is vague, but it's clearly that of a man.

From the corner, a voice begins speaking in a deep, inhuman whisper, "This is your last chance, servant. Fail me again, and I will purge you from my legions. I'll leave you to the tyrant's will." A low, ominous hum fills the room, and the lights flicker for a moment before returning to normal. As they do, the snake and the figure vanish, leaving the corpse motionless on the table.

After a few minutes, the mortician returns. He studies a set of documents as he makes his way toward his desk. The man retakes his seat, grabs his sandwich from earlier, and takes a bite as he starts busying himself on the computer.

The mortician clatters away on the keyboard for a moment; he leans in close, squinting at the screen. After several minutes, he sighs and tilts his head to both sides to stretch his neck. Then he stands up and meanders toward the newest body.

The mortician stands over the man for a moment; he's looking down at a chart that's attached to a clipboard near the head of the body. After studying it for several seconds, he walks to the cart of instruments. He runs his finger over them in a row and selects a medium-sized scalpel.

The mortician reapproaches the dead man with caution. He eyes the body strangely as he moves to the man's side. He readies the scalpel for incision, placing the blade high on the man's chest. The mortician glares at him for a moment longer, then shakes his head, bringing himself back to his current task.

As the mortician presses his blade against the dead flesh, the eyes of the corpse suddenly jolt open. I am filled with life once again—it courses through me like a virus. Anger and hostility fill my gaze while I glare at the horrified man standing over me.

The mortician is frozen; he tries to speak, but the words will not come. As he tries slowly backing away, I shoot my hand up and grab him by the wrist. He drops his scalpel and begins struggling against me, but he cannot break my grasp. He's using his free hand to try to pull away, but it's of no use, I have him.

I sit up on the gurney, placing my feet upon the floor. I am rejuvenated, feeling stronger than ever as I stand up and force him against the steel countertop. He is bent backwards against the metal, knocking over a stack of paper and a few glass vials. He strikes my chest several times ineffectually. His panic pulses once he feels my supremacy.

Then I place my hand on his throat and start squeezing. His eyes become bloodshot while he struggles to breathe. The man's face is flushed red as he continues fighting against me. In less than a minute, he's turning purple, and his struggle soon diminishes. He can do no more. I release my hold and then grab the nearly unconscious man by the hair.

I begin bashing his head against the refrigerator next to the countertop. His head hangs loosely on his neck as I ram it against the steel over and over again. He begins bleeding after several iterations. Then I draw him back and look into his eyes. I honestly can't tell if he's alive or dead, but I do not care. I am done with him, so I drop my hold, and the man collapses like dead weight upon the floor.

I stand brooding over him for a moment as my consciousness floods back into me. Only a single image flashes through my mind—*her*. I can see only her. The vision nearly paralyzes me as I turn and stumble toward the door. It seems my balance hasn't quite caught up with me yet. I leave a wet handprint of thick, sticky blood on the wall as I catch myself from falling. My mouth hangs open as I breathe heavily. *I can taste you.*

I glance over and see a row of scalpels sitting on a nearby tray. I take one of them and put it in my pocket. Then I finish collecting myself before making my way to the double doors. I push them open and head down the long hallway toward the exit.

II.

Café on Main

February 6, 2025

1:00 p.m.

Amara and Cynthia are exiting a small downtown café. They walk through a set of glass doors, then approach a set of covered tables outside. They're both dressed warmly; the midday sun hides behind the thin gray clouds hanging above. The pair of them stop once they reach the first open table; they sit beneath its green umbrella. Cynthia eases herself down, still cautious of her injuries.

They sip their freshly made coffee as they settle into their seats. Amara examines the passersby carrying out their Sunday leisure. "Thanks for meeting me," she says, turning to Cynthia. Amara's humble smile and gentle tone exude a private gratitude.

"I don't know who else I could talk to about all this," she continues. Amara chuckles nervously and shakes her head. "Anyone at the station would think I was crazy. But it's him, I know it is." She pauses and looks away from Cynthia. "You were right. There's something about him, something supernatural. It's evil that gives him life."

Cynthia reflects on all this for a moment before responding, "You don't think it's over yet?"

"I'm not sure..." Amara replies.

Cynthia sighs. "I wish they'd just cremate him and be done with it." The pair of them exchange half-hearted smiles. Cynthia hesitates before asking, "You don't still have that cross I gave you, do you?"

"I'm sorry, I meant to bring it. I'll make sure I get it back to you soon, though."

"Thanks, I'd appreciate it. I have some others, but I'd love to have it back. It was my grandmother's."

"I won't forget," Amara says, nodding with her beverage in hand.

A moment of silence passes between them. "Normally, I wouldn't be the type to ask..." Cynthia begins reluctantly. "But would you like to go to church with me tonight?"

Amara shifts her gaze, considering the proposition. "It's not something I usually do. I haven't been since I was young," she replies, looking off absently. "But after everything that's happened, I don't see how I can say no."

The two women swap polite smiles as a feeling of togetherness envelops them.

Chapter Twelve

I.

Saint Andrew's Catholic Church

February 6, 2025

6:30 p.m.

Evening dusk has begun settling around the city. Amara and Cynthia walk together toward the entrance of a large, ornate church. Its name is displayed on a small wooden sign and surrounded by flowers upon the lawn. The exterior is a faded white stone. The entrance is flanked by two staircases with a dark set of double doors at the top and another at the bottom.

Mighty oak trees surround the church and nearly reach the top of its proud structure. The Virgin Mary is carved into the center of the building above the door with her hand outstretched. She's flanked by two decorative windows; a large flower is etched into the stone above her.

Cynthia and Amara climb the stairs as they take in the beauty of their surroundings. They reach the open door, and a clergyman in a dark purple robe greets them. They smile and nod as they make their way into the lengthy foyer. Thick white pillars flank them on either side, and the ceilings reach up several stories. The chapel doors are open, and the other congregants are already making their way inside.

They walk into the chapel and see three long rows of polished cherry pews. The room's faded red carpet contrasts starkly with its pristine white walls. Stained glass windows are placed all along the right side of the room. Amara studies them as they walk along the aisle toward their seats.

Up ahead, she sees a stained glass portrait of Adam and Eve on the wall behind the altar. A dark blue sky oppresses them. A leafy branch hangs just within their reach. Adam looks away from Eve with his head hanging low. Eve holds the fruit from the tree in her hand and calmly implores him to partake. All the while, the cunning serpent rests upon the leafy branch overhead. His tongue flicks while he watches them with hunger.

Amara has trouble taking her eyes off the large stained glass ahead. She draws her gaze once she notices that Cynthia is heading down one of the rows. She claims her seat, and Amara takes one next to her on the pew.

The detective glances around and examines the people filing inside. She studies her surroundings further, noticing a large set of crimson velvet curtains hanging near the altar; they're tied with ornate yellow rope and tower over the platform. She sees the horizontal lines running all along the walls, drawing her eyes to the ceiling above. Decadent crystal chandeliers hang in rows along the aisles. A large pipe organ sits to the right of the stage. An elderly man in a black suit sits behind it; he plays gentle, welcoming notes as the congregants continue filing in.

After a few moments of idle chatter, the organist stops his melody, and a middle-aged priest walks toward the altar. His jet-black hair is slicked back; he glides with a sense of prominence. His white vestments and black stole exude purity and strength.

The priest comes to the podium and begins flipping through a large red Bible in the center as he waits for the room's silence. "My friends," he begins, scanning the room with somber eyes, "we live through cold and wicked times. The world around us can be so vacuous, so dangerous. We need only to turn on the news to see the terrible things that man does...and all the harm we give one another."

He locks eyes with Amara before continuing, "But we must not despair. We can *never* accept this world's hopelessness during troubled times. For Ephesians 6:12 warns us that 'our struggle is *not* against flesh and blood, but against the rulers, against the *authorities,* against the powers of this dark world, and against the spiritual forces of evil in the heavenly realms.'"

The priest allows his words to sink in before he continues. "We must always remember that our spiritual journey is a *battle*...and that the Lord will provide everything that we need to conquer our adversary. Because in Luke 10:19, scripture tells us that God gives us the power to tread on serpents and scorpions, and over *all* the power of the enemy...and that with this power, nothing shall hurt us."

"Our faith renews us, no matter what evil may come, and no matter how surrounded we may feel. We shall never become pawns in our enemy's hands, so long as we turn to Him. Because when we rely on God, He becomes our avenger. He settles all scores. And Satan's wrath can only ever be overcome by the force of good in our world."

He pauses for another moment, allowing his words to enter their minds. He shifts his gaze across the congregation, meeting their curious little stares with confidence. Amara watches him pensively as the man continues his impassioned sermon.

II.

Saint Andrew's Catholic Church

February 6, 2025

7:45 p.m.

"So, what'd you think?" Cynthia asks casually. She flashes a hopeful smile as she and Amara are exiting through the main doors. They pause at the top of the stairs.

"I think…it's exactly what I needed to hear. It was good to get out too, helped take my mind off everything. Maybe I should come more often. Might make the job a little easier."

The rest of the congregants begin passing them by and descending the white stone staircase. "I'd love to do it again sometime," Cynthia offers in a friendly tone.

"So would I," Amara replies.

Cynthia nods. "Well, I'm going to confession now, but I'll give you a call soon."

"I'd like that."

The pair of them part ways with awkward smiles. Cynthia heads back inside the tall set of double doors. Amara starts down the staircase but pauses after taking the first step down. She looks as though there's still something she wants to say as she glances back at Cynthia. But her friend vanishes from sight quickly, and the opportunity has now passed. Cynthia's inside the church; she walks slowly through the foyer as Amara departs with her private burden.

III.

Saint Andrew's Catholic Church
February 6, 2025
7:45 p.m.

A cold, nascent rain starts pattering against my skin as I come upon the church. Its powerful white structure towers over me and stands starkly against the waning twilight. I'm still wearing the cop's uniform, the pants and boots, anyway. The blood from my injuries has caked and dried upon my flesh. My face is barely recognizable beneath the hardened red clumps. I am *filth*, obstinate and unrefined.

I approach an exterior wrought iron gate on the side of the building. It's short enough to jump over and has nothing placed over the top to stop me. The rain starts watering the dirt next to the gate, muddying my boots as I step into it.

I clutch onto the top of the gate before squatting down. I jump, press myself up to the top, then swing my legs over to get to the other side. I land on a paved path between two doors with a loud thud. And now, I must make a choice. I select the door on the left because it seems to lead into the main body of the church.

As I tug on the rustic green door's metal handle, I notice that it's padlocked from the outside. Time to get creative. I glance into the gated courtyard between the two doors, noticing a little display of stones gathered near a tree in the center. I open the gate, walk inside, and take one of the stones. It's large, nearly the size of my forearm. I raise the stone overhead and bash the lock repeatedly until it clatters to the walkway below.

Now that I've taken the lock off, I open the creaking door and walk inside. All is quiet as I enter, and the overhead lights are rather dim. It's so desolate; this entrance must be far from the chapel. I peek around the corner after stepping down a short flight of stairs. The walls are brown and largely uncovered. Ahead, there's a long hallway with several doors at the end.

I begin walking down the hallway, listening intently while I step with caution. I hear hushed movement up ahead, so I dip into one of the doorway slots and peek my head out again. Someone is inside one of the offices down the hall. After a moment, I see a priest walking slowly from one room into another that's directly in front of it. I hear the shuffling of papers inside before he emerges again.

The balding, middle-aged man turns from the office and begins walking down the hall. He's staring down at a set of papers while pacing toward me. I watch him from the shadows, waiting patiently until he enters the doorway across from mine.

The man pauses once he reaches the wooden double doors. He's reading something from his documents and completely unaware as I move toward him. I'm just a few feet behind the priest when he places a hand on the door's handle. He stops and turns his head slowly, sensing some presence there. But before he spots me, I grab the purple stole that's hanging from his neck.

He quickly grabs at the fabric once he starts to choke, but I've already pulled it too tight. I draw him in closer and pull as hard as I can. He tries slapping at my hands, then attempts to reach for my eyes, but it's all no use. This feeble man was mine the second I took hold. He starts to collapse, so

I press him against the wall. I maintain my hold and continue pulling until his cheeks are flushed red.

I draw him back and study the man's face. His body sags beneath the stole that's wrapped around his neck; his eyes are empty and fixed on the floor. I unwrap the garment from his throat and shove his vacant body onto the ground. Suddenly, I feel rejuvenated, holding the stole out before me. The lights shine upon it as I examine the golden stitching and a pair of decorative crosses embroidered along the sides.

"Washed in the blood of the Lamb," I utter, grinning with my head held low. The words hypnotize me as I place the garment around my shoulders. I let it settle around my neck and stretch it out front. I'm feeling joyful and relaxed, but I cannot bask for long because my mission draws me back to my senses.

I walk to the door, open it, and then glance around. It's very quiet. I walk down a short hallway and come to another door at the end. Then I press my ear to the wood and listen for several seconds before creaking it open.

I'm inside the chapel now, so I must have been closer than I thought. I spot the confessional booth and scurry toward it. Then I peek over the corner. Footsteps. The wonderful sound of heels clacking against a wooden floor fills my ears—and then I see her coming in from the lobby.

Cynthia starts heading down the aisle with her head down; she's absorbed in some formal reflection. I smile to myself as I slink back into hiding.

IV.

Saint Andrew's Catholic Church

February 6, 2025

8:00 p.m.

Cynthia approaches the confessional. It's an ornate wooden structure with columns carved along the sides; there's an hourglass post running through the middle and twin crosses are etched into the doors. Cynthia crosses herself with her right hand while stopping in front of it. She stares at the box with solemn eyes before entering through the left-hand door.

Cynthia closes the heavy wooden door behind her. She sets her purse down and then kneels in a small leather booth next to the window; it's an opaque material that gives her complete anonymity. Cynthia takes a moment longer to clear her mind. Then she closes her eyes and begins praying quietly.

She mutters to herself for another thirty seconds before the door on the other side opens. I come inside and take my seat in silence.

Cynthia waits a few seconds for me to settle in before saying, "Bless me, Father, for I have sinned."

She can see nothing from the other side of the screen. The hopefulness in her voice excites me to no end as I think of all the things I'd love to do to her. I lean back against the wall, smiling as I look down on my purple stole. I stretch it in the air; my fingers caress the little crosses down by the bottom. "Tell me your sins, my child," I reply in a low, flat tone.

"It has been three weeks since my last confession," Cynthia pauses before continuing, "I had road rage and cursed at another driver. I took a few things from work, and I didn't help a homeless man when he asked. Times have been hard lately, and I just feel so...guilty." She shakes her head in silence.

"Go on," I tell her with a warm inflection.

"I've been unforgiving toward others," Cynthia admits grudgingly. "There was this man, an evil, terrible man. He hurt people. And when I saw that he died, I couldn't help but feel relieved. I hated him. I know I'm not supposed to, but I absolutely hated him."

After Cynthia relieves herself of her guilt, there's a long pause. I can hear her breath coming slow and rhythmic. She awaits my absolution.

"So, what you're telling me is...you've been a very, very bad girl," I answer, my voice coming dark and melodic. I arch my eyebrows and grin from the other side.

Cynthia is taken aback by my answer. She's visibly uncomfortable and begins shifting on her knees. She stands up from the booth and then sits on a chair behind her. She hesitates for a moment before continuing. "I'm just not sure what to do, Father."

I allow the tension to build between us for several seconds before answering, "Don't worry, princess, daddy will take care of you."

Cynthia has gone from tense to frightened. She goes to look through the screen, moving her head back and forth for a better angle, but can see nothing at all from the other side. Unbeknownst to her, I'm drawing the scalpel that I took from the morgue. I take it from my pocket, place my thumb on the handle, and stand up slowly.

Then I draw my arm back as I prepare to strike. I listen to all her silent suspicions for a few seconds longer before I plunge the knife forward. The blade tears through the screen and my fist punches out to the other side.

I slice her deeply across the cheek. Cynthia shrinks back, clutching her face. She begins wailing as the shock of it hits her. She recoils on the chair before coming to her senses. Then she sees my hand reaching through the hole. I'm stabbing at her with wild enthusiasm.

This ignites her terror. Cynthia screams loudly as she stands from her chair and goes for the door. But I am already exiting through mine. I see her door opening and I kick it shut. Inside, she's panicking and trying to hold the door closed to stop my advance. I reach for the handle and tug on it. It lurches forward a few times, but she keeps it held in place.

I exert myself and yank the door open. Cynthia nearly tumbles out as I rip the handle from her grasp. She tries to run past me, but I grab her by the shoulder and shove her back inside the box. The door's still ajar. I step inside, and now I'm hovering over her while she cowers on the seat below.

Cynthia raises her hands to shield her face. I slash into her forearms, and she cries out. I continue raising and lowering the blade in a wild frenzy. The scalpel cuts into her skin with ease; it leaves deep puncture wounds and long, bloody trails. She continues screaming and crying beneath my onslaught until there's nothing left.

Her blood is splattered along the walls. It runs beneath my boots and begins pooling on the floor inside the confessional. Cynthia is frozen in her chair; she's peppered with small incisions, leaking from her wounds.

I stare down at my covered arms. My entire body is stained with luscious, warm red. It drips down my shirtless torso and collects on the stole that's still hanging from my neck. I'm staring at her and breathing heavily while my shoulders rise and fall. My steady gaze spreads unflinching hatred throughout the room; it crawls up the ceilings and stretches into the darkest corners.

This fixation persists until I hear a metal door creaking open outside. I step out of the booth to investigate. A priest has entered the room. He's elderly with thin white hair on the sides. His jaw hangs open as he gapes at me in confusion. He's clutching a Bible in his right hand. I'm still holding onto the scalpel and drenched in blood as I stare back at him.

A wide, menacing smile spreads across my lips. "Run, run, little lamb," I say, taking a few paces toward him. He's shaking as he drops the book by his side and then rushes for the door. My inhuman laughter returns, and I cackle like a diseased hyena. My eyes glow a faint blue in the church's dim light.

After watching the man flee, I turn back and spot a series of lit candles near the altar. I walk toward them and pick up a standing candelabra. I admire the trembling flames as I clutch it in my hand. Then I glance to my right and take stock of the altar as a plan forms within my mind.

Long velvet curtains hang down to the floor on both sides of the altar. I approach them with the candelabra in hand. Then I bend down next to the curtain on the right and touch it with the flame. It takes a few seconds to catch, but when it does, the fire spreads across the breadth of the curtain and begins traveling up quickly. After seeing that it's caught, I walk to the curtain on the left and set the flaming candle down on top of it. I leave it on the ground and begin walking away as the flames spread.

As I'm heading out, the fire begins lapping at the tall ceilings above. Nearby fixtures start burning as well. The flames are massive due to the sheer size of the burning curtains; it all starts spreading wondrously.

Time to go find that wandering priest, I think to myself. I head toward the exit while burning debris begins falling from the ceiling.

Chapter Thirteen

I.

Detective Cruz's Apartment

February 6, 2025

9:20 p.m.

Amara sits on a red couch in her apartment in front of the television. She's wearing jeans and a white shirt while she rests with her feet next to her on the couch. The news is on, but Amara pays little attention as she flips through the pages of *The Serpent's Call*. The television anchor prattles on about weather and traffic conditions while she hunts for answers.

Amara comes to a section entitled "Continuing Resurrection." The paragraph beneath it details how an evil force, once brought back to life, may continue reemerging until it is laid to rest through a banishing spell. She glances over at the table in front of the couch, examining the Ziploc bag full of the dirt taken from the dead man's boots. Cynthia's small wooden cross is laid to the side of it.

Amara places her finger below the banishing spell. She studies its instructions and commits them to memory. "For best results," she reads aloud, "sprinkle the mixture in front of your enemy's door to force him from your community." She skims the part again where it states, "Your adversary's presence will vex you no longer; he will rot and perish from your world." She looks up from the book, glances around the room, and then closes it shut.

Amara sets the book down on the coffee table in front of her couch. She grabs the cross and the Ziploc bag and then makes her way toward the kitchen. She places the items on the counter before opening a small cabinet full of spices.

Amara pulls out a shaker of cayenne pepper and then studies the cabinet's contents for a moment. "Sassafras, sassafras," she whispers to herself. Amara reaches into the back and appears surprised when she has it. She sets it down next to the cayenne pepper and then moves a jar of coffee grounds beside them.

The detective opens the Ziploc bag and then starts mixing the ingredients together. She shakes the contents of the bag around, watching as the individual powders mesh together. Amara sighs as she looks down at the cross. She places the bag on the counter and then picks it up, clutching the wood and running her thumb along the face of it.

Amara gazes at it thoughtfully for a moment before noticing the little jar that's affixed to the center with a band. It's small, no more than fingernail in size. She unscrews the jar's tiny lid while she considers her options. Amara shakes her head, lowering the jar to the open bag. She scoops a little of the mixture inside the jar and closes the lid again.

Something on the news catches Amara's attention as she's putting her spices away. She sets the items down and then walks toward the television. "And now, breaking news out of Fulton County, where Saint Andrew's Catholic Church has been engulfed in flames for roughly the last hour.

Fulton County Fire Department is reporting that they've found at least one dead inside while they've struggled to contain the blaze."

Amara's mind begins racing as she stares at the footage from the burning church. "Investigators have yet to establish the identity of this individual as it is still an active scene," the voice carries on. Amara continues studying the television until her concentration is broken by the ringing of her phone. After a few seconds, she manages to pull herself away.

"Hello," she answers in a flat tone as she studies the unfolding events. Amara listens for about twenty seconds while a voice on the other end delivers a hurried, long-winded message. "Got it. I'm on my way," she answers at last. Amara ends the call and lets the phone hang by her hip for a moment as she watches the fiery images on the screen.

She snaps out of her trance and then grabs her pistol, the Ziploc bag, and the cross. Amara throws on a leather jacket before rushing out of her apartment.

II.

Saint Andrew's Catholic Church

February 6, 2025

9:50 p.m.

Amara stares in amazement as she drives toward the scene of the flaming church. Her expression is incredulous and frozen. The proud edifice is smoldering before her as she parks her car in front of the building. She watches while the smoke drifts across the empty nighttime sky.

Amara steps out of her car, pulls her badge from her jacket pocket, and starts advancing toward the church. It's a good hundred feet away. Before she reaches it, she's stopped by two officers as she crosses under the caution tape. She shows them her badge, but they explain that the fire isn't contained yet, and they're not letting anyone inside.

"They've gotten most of it, but it'll still be a while before anyone goes in," the young officer reports.

Amara nods and then turns away. She begins walking back to her car. Then she stops and stares at the ground for a moment. Her eyes shrink and her forehead wrinkles. "I know how to find you…" she whispers. Amara hurries the rest of the distance to her car. She hops inside, cranks the ignition, and speeds to a new destination with rekindled resolve.

III.

Eastview Cemetery

February 6, 2025

10:10 p.m.

Amara pulls to a stop as her headlights shine upon the cemetery gate. She cuts her ignition but leaves the headlights on as she steps out of her car. The absorbed detective takes stock of the nearly barren graveyard as her hand rests atop the doorframe.

Amara spots a man a few hundred feet away. He's wearing a dark red flannel shirt and jeans. He carries a shovel while he walks toward a small building with the exterior lights on. The man sets the shovel down by the doorway before walking inside and switching off the lights. Then Amara reaches inside her car and grabs her flashlight, the cross, and the Ziploc bag.

She places the cross and the bag inside her jacket pocket, turns on her flashlight, and starts walking toward the opening of the gate. After she crosses through, the detective walks for a few minutes along a narrow path leading to a row of headstones on the outer edge of the cemetery.

A harsh wind blows as she continues making her way through the dark necropolis. Amara spots a stray dog up ahead, but it turns a corner, and she loses sight of it. Then she comes to a set of headstones before reaching the back gate. All seems quiet and undisturbed, except for one plot that lies exposed between two others.

Amara stops ahead of the plot and then takes a few paces toward it. She stares at the vacant hole with no expression. Patches of dirt are cast unevenly around the edges. She glances inside and sees that the casket remains. Its wooden lid is broken and moved off to one side. She shines her light within the grave, seeing dozens of spiders and roaches scurry across the cheap velvet lining.

Amara glances behind her toward the small building. There's no movement; she's all alone, save for the aimless sounds of night. Amara removes the Ziploc bag from her pocket. She folds her lips and looks down at the bag while running her finger along the plastic exterior. A few seconds pass in eerie silence while she stares at it broodingly.

The detective opens the bag and then stands directly over the grave. She turns the bag on its side and allows its contents to sift out to the earth below. Amara continues staring into the hole and pulls a slip of paper from her pocket. She shines her light upon the paper, studying its words. The little heading above reads, "Banishing Evil Entities."

"Behold...I shall be not afraid, but trust in the stars of Heaven," she reads aloud, "Its righteous constellations give thee no light, and the sun will starve thy malice. At eventide, trouble, but before morning, ruin."

Amara glances around nervously. "Come on," she whispers. She becomes fidgety as the seconds turn to minutes. Amara looks to the ground and sighs, but as she gazes up, the night sky has grown substantially darker. The idle chatter of her surroundings ceases. She's focusing on the grave when a loud cracking sound breaks the silence behind her. A large branch from an apple tree has tumbled to the earth about fifty feet away.

Amara glares at the fallen branch for several seconds before turning back to the grave. She glances down at the small piece of paper in her hand. Then she turns her flashlight off and stares absently into the night sky. After a moment, the detective crumples up the paper and gazes out the back gate.

Amara reopens her grasp on the paper, and as she does, small flames begin to skirt the corners of it. Little embers start devouring the edges while she stares with amazement. Ash begins collecting in her palm as the flaming note is carried off by the wind.

She watches the fading flames scurry toward the apple tree behind her. It lands atop the fallen branch, sits for a few seconds, and then bursts into a tall, transient flame. A figure appears. The fire shrinks quickly but continues burning the branch as smoke starts to rise.

Amara squints her eyes, straining to see from her distance in the low light. But she knows who stands before her. She knew I'd come; she'd been expecting me all along. I can feel her heart beating faster. I can taste her quickening breath.

I'm leaning against the apple tree with a black rose in hand. I'm wearing an all-black suit with polished leather shoes. My skin is pale and clean. I twirl the flower slowly with my eyes closed. My hair hangs in my face as I lean down and breathe the aroma. Then I reopen my eyes and grin at the glaring detective.

IV.

Eastview Cemetery

February 6, 2025

10:20 p.m.

The dwindling fire crackles as the branch begins smoldering next to me on the ground. I inhale the rose's scent a final time before tossing the flower onto the pyre. The dark aura nourishes my body while it forms around me.

As I glance back at Amara, I notice that she's drawn her pistol. She holds it at the ready by her side. I step toward her with a warm and gentle smile. She identifies herself as Atlanta PD. Then she shouts her commands, ordering me to stop where I am.

"Why stop," I ask, "when we could be together?" I gesture outwardly with my arms as I continue pacing toward her. She fires once at the ground; I smile as I look down at the dirt being kicked up by my feet. She orders me to stop a second time, but I will not.

A door slams in the distance. It's the groundskeeper emerging from his little hut. He stares with heightened concern as he stands cautiously on the front steps of the small building. The man has a cellphone in his right hand. He begins to dial.

Amara and I draw our eyes back to each other. I continue stepping toward her. I'm about twenty feet away when she fires again. The bullet tears through my shoulder, but it's barely enough to slow me down. She continues shouting at me as she fires another round. It strikes me in the chest, and that halts me for a moment. I double over as I catch my breath.

I wheeze and groan for a couple of seconds, but then it's back up again. My breath becomes ragged as I clutch my chest with a strained smile. "Was that helpful?" I ask, turning my head toward her.

Amara shouts in anger as she fires several more rounds into me. The bullets tear bloody holes into my shirt. My body twists and trembles with each impact. She continues firing until I collapse.

Amara fires twice more as I lie motionless on the ground. She studies my inert body from the distance. Then she returns the pistol to her holster and glances over at the approaching groundskeeper.

He's speechless while he creeps toward us. Amara draws her badge and holds it up as he comes closer. "Detective Cruz, Atlanta PD," she calls out to him.

The groundskeeper approaches me with caution. His mouth hangs open as he leans over to get a better look. "Is he dead?" the man asks finally.

Amara clenches her jaw as she stares down at my body. "I don't know," she replies after a few seconds.

The groundskeeper continues watching me for a moment. "I already called for help...Looks like maybe he's still breathing." The sympathetic idiot hovers over me, squats down, and places two fingers upon my neck.

"Stop!" Amara shouts.

"I need to check his pulse," the man replies.

"Don't, just get away from him," she warns.

But her warning comes too late. The man stares at her with confusion as he feels my neck pulsing through his fingers. As he's looking away, I reach my hand to his throat and draw my bowie knife from a sheath that's tucked into my waistband. His wide, frozen eyes glare at me as I squeeze his neck. I pull him toward me and plunge the blade into his sternum; within seconds, blood trickles from the edge of his lips.

As I continue stabbing the man, Amara draws her pistol and aims. But she doesn't have the shot, and I know it. The man acts as my personal buffer as I drain the life from his body. His flowing blood stains my hands and suit. It covers my neck and spatters my face.

As I throw him off me, I can see the pistol shaking in Amara's hand. She's incredulous and breathing heavily while she watches me rise to my feet. I'm standing upright by the time she fires again. The bullet catches my shoulder and jerks me back for a second.

Amara fires once more, and it strikes me in the gut. I'm jolted back but recompose myself quickly. I stagger as I clench the knife and dab my finger into the open wound. The warm blood swallows my finger; I raise it to my lips to lick it clean.

"Not this time, my love," I tell her, shaking my head as I gaze upon her softly. "I won't be stopped." The dark aura hangs above my head. It surrounds my figure with its tall, menacing shadow. I feel utterly invulnerable. All Amara can do now is slow me down, and she can see this—so she runs.

I lurch toward her at a measured pace. Amara glances over her shoulder several times as she flees. She's heading up a path toward a mausoleum. It's a stone structure with dark gray pillars, a black metal door with golden etching, and a large window out front. The surrounding exterior lights are quite dim. She flings the door open and rushes inside as I continue advancing calmly.

Amara is fumbling with the door's handle as I approach. She reaches for the lock in the dark before grasping that it's not there. I place my hand upon the knob and pull. Amara spots me and pulls her handle from the other side. She's tugging with all her might as she stares with petrified eyes.

Amara is breathing heavily, exerting herself. I can't help but marvel at the sight of her fear as I toy with her on the other side. I can tear this door down any time I'd like. I want her under the illusion of safety, savoring the prospect of her survival. But I have you now, little mouse. You're backed into my corner and trapped in my domain.

The dark aura surrounds me and begins seeping into the cracks of the mausoleum. It stifles the air around her with a horrid, rotting stench. I pull the door hard; the knob nearly slips from her grip. Amara draws her pistol in desperation, takes a step back, and fires several times into the door's window.

The bullets cut the glass and pierce my skin. The barrage she releases sends me back several paces. I'm stumbling around when she opens the door and fires three more shots into my chest. I've taken to one knee. I'm gasping and sweating as I wipe my brow and glance up at her.

Amara wastes no time, skirting past me cautiously. She departs down the path as I catch my breath. I watch her run toward the cemetery as I raise myself back up with great effort.

Instead of heading back to my grave, Amara runs into the more densely populated area on the right. Another mausoleum is in the center of the section; it's flanked by several rows of upright headstones and obelisks. She dashes away from the path and begins running through the cemetery. Her feet slap against the small, timeworn markers while she strides.

Amara glances behind her and sees me keeping a steady pace about a hundred feet away. But she turns around too late, and her knee catches on a low standing cross as she passes by. Amara grimaces and cries out in pain. She nearly falls over but manages to keep her balance.

The detective clutches her leg while she moves at a reduced pace. She's hobbling along as best she can as I start closing the distance between us. I can hear her grunts growing louder as I draw nearer.

Amara reaches the top of a small hill. The change in landscape causes her shaky leg to buckle. She trips and then falls to one knee. Amara cries out as she tumbles a few feet to the bottom. Panicked, she looks up, and there I am—just ten feet away with the knife hanging by my side. She groans loudly while forcing herself back onto one knee. Amara draws her pistol and points it at me. It shakes within her fearful grasp.

Amara is entirely frozen as she stares into my empty gaze. Before she can fire again, I lunge at her and jab the blade into her shoulder. Then I watch her face contort while she reels from the pain. The knife sits idly inside her flesh as I consume her agony. We are together now, locked in our private world of darkness. I raise my free hand to her chin and lift her head to meet my gaze. "Surrender to me...and let it all go," I beckon in a low whisper.

When she refuses to look at me, I twist the knife inside her shoulder. Her face wrenches in anguish. Amara strains under the awful tension happening inside of her. She raises her pistol and draws back with the knife still inside her flesh. As I reach my hand out to hers, she fires upon me once.

The gun clicks empty, but the single shot cuts through two of my fingers. They tumble to the earth below. I am left with two bloody knubs on my right ring and pinky. Blood flows from the wounds while I gnash my teeth and glare at the protruding bone. The heavy gore looks black upon my flesh under the moon's dim light. Amara stares in awe, placing her empty gun back inside the holster.

She pulls back as she draws the knife from her skin. Then she turns and tries getting back onto her feet. But before she can stand, I club her across the back with my bloody hand. The impact knocks her off balance, and she falls back onto the grass below. Amara grunts and mumbles as she begins crawling away from me.

I'm still unsteady on my feet and struggling to catch my breath as I stagger toward her. Amara paces forward on her knees and elbows. She shrieks when I grab a fistful of her jacket and start turning her over onto her side. The detective slaps me hard in the face while struggling to break my grasp.

I drop my knee on top of Amara as I force her onto her back. Then I take hold of her quarrelsome hands and straddle her near the waist. The blood from my right hand covers her chest and neck once I place my fingers upon her throat.

Amara is beginning to fade beneath me as something catches her eye. It's a large statue several feet away: a somber angel of weathered stone stands near a bench; she's reaching down and picking leaves from a large plant in the garden. Amara stares for several seconds longer before her eyes start to flutter.

I'm pressing as hard as I can on her throat while I lean in close. Our faces are only about six inches apart now. I gaze down at her longingly; there's a deep sense of finality in the air. The short, muffled sounds escaping her throat are barely audible as I look up to the moonlit sky.

The detective begins shifting as I take my eyes off her. She's still holding onto the knife; it's concealed along the side of her leg. I draw a deep breath as I close my eyes and continue applying pressure. Then she grabs hold of my hands while they're placed upon her throat. As I begin to open my eyes, I feel the knife plunge into the side of my neck.

My eyes grow wide as I draw my hands from her throat. My neck begins hemorrhaging, and I'm struggling to breathe as I clutch myself. The wound leaks upon us both. My black shirt is dampened; her face and torso are splotched with warm, flowing red.

I try to force myself back onto my feet, but I feel dizzy and uneven. My head bobs as I press against the wound. It's no use, I feel myself fading. Amara begins gasping for air, and my body starts shaking as I raise a hand toward the blade that's stuck in my neck.

The weight becomes too much to bear; my body slumps involuntarily. I feel Amara shifting beneath me as she starts to catch her breath. She begins hoisting my lethargic body to one side with her legs. Then I teeter to the ground and land on my side.

My lips are opening and closing in a tender, misguided sort of way. I can draw only short, shallow breaths; my chest barely rises with every pained motion. I lie upon my side, staring jadedly at the angel statue as I bleed on the ground. Amara continues catching her breath next to me. After several seconds, our eyes meet, and we writhe together.

About a minute passes before Amara gathers herself. She sits up slowly, straining with her arms. Her breath is still ragged as she sits across from me, gaping in disbelief. Her hand trembles as she places her palm upon the earth.

The detective crawls a few paces closer to me. I turn my head toward her slowly. Then she mounts herself on top of me and stares into my enfeebled eyes. Amara takes hold of the knife that's still protruding from my neck. I shake my head. "Don't," I try to tell her, but my voice will not come. She draws the blade from my neck as I choke out a wet gasp.

After Amara slides the gleaming metal from my wound, blood pumps in little spurts onto the grass. My head slumps on the ground, and I look at her with defeat in my eyes. I try to move my hands, but there is nothing to be done. I am immobilized.

Amara lifts the blade overhead, shrieking as she drives it upon me. She presses down with both hands, putting her weight atop the handle. I can barely keep my eyes open as she raises it again. Amara sticks me in the chest but doesn't dwell on the blow this time. She continues stabbing in a wild frenzy, cutting me across the neck, chest, and face.

Then she lifts it once more, jabbing me just beneath the collar bone. Her hand lingers there while she studies me with a sense of tired anticipation. Five seconds pass with no motion, then ten. With no signs of life, she looks up to the moon, breathing a small sigh of relief.

V.

Eastview Cemetery

February 6, 2025

10:35 p.m.

A few seconds later, Amara's hopeful gaze is broken by the feeling of movement beneath her. *It cannot be*, her eyes say to mine as she turns toward me. But there I am, lifting my head, and struggling to rise again.

Amara places a hand against my rising shoulder. I can feel her pulse quickening; I can taste her fear. The detective's eyes grow wide as she begins to panic. Amara scans the graveyard anxiously, searching for a way out. Then something dawns on her as she reaches into her jacket pocket.

And there it is—the cross. I can feel its weight upon me already. Whatever she's treated it with stifles the air around me. Forgiveness, love, community—they fill my lungs with their awful effusion. Their unwanted presence looms with a vile stench, and I feel utterly tormented.

Amara's hands shake as she holds the relic before her. She closes her eyes in desperation and presses the wood against my forehead. I cry out when it touches my skin. Then she leans forward, keeping me pinned to the dreadful earth below.

My eyes flash blue once the wood is upon me, but they fade quickly, turning to empty, black marble. It feels like hot steel is branding me into submission. The little vial attached to it cuts a hole in my forehead. *I hate it with every fiber of my being.* I fight as best I can with her weight on top of me, but the oppressive force is surging into my brain, poisoning me rapidly. I can feel it, I am withering.

Amara feels my movement beneath her stop. Her breath grows ragged as she stares into my bleeding eyes. They pour a thick, black sludge. It streams across my face before dripping onto the grass. Then she draws back, removing the cross from my forehead.

I can feel my flesh beginning to rot. It starts losing its substance while I grow a shade paler. My memories take me back to the courthouse again. I feel the sting of her bullet lodging into my shoulder. It's all becoming so distended and amplified. The old wound begins to smolder. It starts tearing a hole in my flesh that grows wider and wider. A stream of smoke pours from the gash as I lie motionless on the ground.

Amara's eyes begin to flutter as she fights to keep them open. She's intoxicated by my death and the dark aura surrounding us. Her vision blurs once its power overtakes her. She breathes the black mist for several seconds before it begins to dissipate.

Amara puts a hand on the ground as she starts falling to the side, but she's not quick enough to catch herself. She falls to the ground next to me. Her head bobs back and forth as she struggles to maintain consciousness. Amara places her hand on my chest, trying to push herself up, but it's useless—she's down and out.

Time stands still with the pair of us cradled against one another. For several minutes, only the whistling of the wind can be heard through the trees above. The dark mass is nearly gone now; it continues drifting across the night sky until it's so thin that it simply disappears.

Epilogue

I.

Eastview Cemetery

February 6, 2025

10:50 p.m.

Amara finally awakens after lying on my chest for several minutes longer. Her arm is still draped across my body as she looks at my corpse with a sense of gloom. Then she glances down at the cross still clutched inside her hand. The gentle moonlight shines upon the symbol as she examines it.

Amara looks toward the angel statue with bleary eyes; she stares into its tranquil gaze as though searching for an answer. She stands to her feet and then looks to the moon, placing the cross back inside her jacket pocket.

Amara casts the same bereft gaze upon me. After a few seconds, she steps in front of my legs. Then she kneels down and takes hold of both feet. Amara strains as she begins tugging on my ankles. They're wrapped along her waist while she begins dragging my corpse.

Step by step, Amara moves my body along the pathway. After about twenty feet, she glances over her shoulder and spots my headstone. Amara pulls me alongside it and then allows my feet to drop. There is no real victory upon her face; there's only silent regret and an empty longing for all that was.

Amara kneels next to my corpse and places a tender hand upon my shoulder. The tired detective reflects on everything that's happened before pushing my body into the grave. It tumbles off the edge as I roll into the earth below. My shell lands inside the open casket, motionless, and sprawled on its side. Cold, empty eyes stare into the wall of the grave.

Amara is shaky on her feet as she towers over the open hole. Taking the cross from her jacket pocket, she hesitates for a moment, and then drops the relic into the grave.

Amara stares into my plot while raising a shaky hand to her wound. The blood has soaked through her white shirt. She studies her coated fingers with incoherent fascination. Then she raises her jacket's collar and finds that her body is drenched on one side.

Amara's energy begins to wane as she trudges toward a nearby headstone. She leans against it and lowers herself to the ground. Her head bobs gently while she casts a tired, mournful gaze to my open grave. Amara continues staring until the weight of her eyelids becomes too great to bear. Her head sags as her body slumps against the stone.

II.

Eastview Cemetery

February 6, 2025

11:10 p.m.

Amara is still unconscious when two paramedics arrive at the cemetery gate. Their ambulance cruises through the grounds with caution. A man and a woman in their mid-thirties pull onto the scene as their flashing lights illuminate the desolate graveyard. Once they reach the guard shack, the driver stops the ambulance. The exterior lampposts provide scarce light to the scene below.

Both paramedics wear solid black uniforms. They scan the area around them as they step out of the vehicle. There's no movement by the shack. The two start heading toward it, but as they do, they spot the dead groundskeeper lying next to cemetery path. His torso is covered in blood from the belly down. They study his vacant expression as they approach.

The female paramedic squats down next to the groundskeeper. Her short blonde hair hangs in her face as she examines him. The other glances down but continues studying the night's strange setting. He draws a small flashlight and shines it on the path ahead.

The thin, light-skinned man gazes with suspicion as he cranes his neck to examine the area. As he strains to see, he spots Amara's hand protruding from the corner of a headstone.

"He's dead," the woman reports, looking to her partner.

"Think we got someone else over here too," the man replies.

She glances to the spot where his light shines and then stands to her feet. The pair of them start down the walkway together. They pick up their pace as they grow closer. Once they reach Amara, the man checks her pulse. "She's stable, but I'm not sure how long we have."

"Let's get the stretcher, then," she replies.

They head off quickly and walk toward the vehicle's rear door. The man opens it and hops inside. He begins drawing out a yellow stretcher. His partner assists him, and the pair of them get it out onto the ground. They move efficiently. In a few seconds, they're back by Amara's side. She's still unconscious when they lower the bed and hoist her up onto it.

The night's tranquility is interrupted by the wailing of police sirens. Their red and blue lights flash through the tall, leafless trees. The paramedics continue strapping Amara to the bed. They raise her up, and the man steps behind it. He starts pushing as the woman guides the stretcher along by its side. They move Amara down the path and then struggle up a small hill toward the ambulance.

As they begin loading her into the vehicle, two uniformed officers approach. They begin asking questions about what happened here. The male paramedic directs them toward the dead man lying on the path. He informs the officer that they must get this woman to the hospital; then he hops inside the driver's seat. The female paramedic jumps in the back with Amara and then closes the door behind them.

After several minutes of riding together, Amara begins to wake. Her eyes open and close as she moves her head without purpose. She peers around cautiously before closing them again. The woman starts asking her questions while Amara struggles to stay awake. The paramedic waits, but no answer comes. Amara drifts off once more, and they ride the rest of the way in silence.

III.

Eastview Cemetery
February 7, 2025
2:15 a.m.

A team of forensic investigators are just now finishing up at the cemetery. They busy themselves in blue windbreakers with yellow lettering on the back. Several of them are still loading the last of their equipment into their black SUV. Once finished, they all hop inside and begin driving away. The red taillights fade into the distance as a cold breeze shakes the yellow caution tape stretched out around the scene.

As they depart, the night sky shifts to endless black. Only thin light coming from a nearby lamppost illuminates the barren graveyard. The dark aura has returned. It trails in from a gentle gust and skirts the ground near my open hole. The dense, black cloud centers itself above my burial plot. It hugs the corners of my grave before descending upon me. The mass swirls inside and then consumes my body in darkness.

After several seconds, the dark wreath begins to disperse. It continues swirling as a snake appears at the center. The powerful serpent rests in a coil atop my chest. "You have utterly failed me," his voice rebukes from the shadows. "You have made your fate, and I will offer no sanctuary." The serpent raises up a few inches, staring intently. His greedy tongue flicks while his head bobs with anticipation.

But I will not be rebuked—for I am not done. As the snake prepares to strike, I seize him by the neck. The serpent hisses and struggles within my grasp, but I far am too strong. He wriggles, he squirms, but it all adds to nothing, for the fate of the worm is now mine.

Then I guide the snake toward my opening mouth. My jaws extend as the serpent grows closer. He tries drawing back, but I continue straining him forward. The snake bites the inside of my cheek. Blood begins spilling from my lips; it runs down my neck and pools on my chest. As the serpent digs his fangs into my soft, pink tissue, I bite into him as well. He jolts forward while I sink my teeth into his body.

I'm clenching my jaw while the serpent continues trying to break free. Then I tear the form asunder, ripping his head from his body as it wriggles in my hand. Putrid black blood empties from the severed tip as it fills my mouth. It starts at the edge of my lips and runs onto my tattered clothes. The vile, flowing substance fills me with life once again.

I bellow with deep hunger into the cold night. I have discarded my master. The black mass works its way around me with an energetic swirl. It plumes at the top of my grave and scatters in all directions as it grazes the earth. It travels a short distance before dissipating into the nighttime air. This will be my moment yet.

But something is tearing from within. I can feel a force fighting itself inside of my organs. It pushes and pulls against me. I groan and cry as I clutch my stomach. Then it begins to rain. The drops come slow and sporadic at first, but it soon gives way to a cold, bitter shower.

Images of my life flash before my eyes as my consciousness is uprooted. Suddenly, I am within myself, inside of my own body. I fumble through wet, slippery organs as I press against the tissue from within. My teeth tear a hole, and I manage to press myself through the dead, pale flesh. I emerge from the center of my old shell. I gaze down upon it; the empty eyes stare into the night sky above.

I am the serpent, and I've become the power now. My new form is mighty. This body is dense, black, and scaled. My head is wide and proud like a cobra's. The cross placed atop my old body crumbles to ash in my presence. I slither up the muddy walls to regain my freedom. Once atop the wet grass, I refocus my purpose.

IV.

Grady Memorial Hospital

February 7, 2025

3:00 a.m.

Amara has been drifting in and out of consciousness for the last few hours. Every time she awakens, a new hangover seems to greet her; it towers overhead, casting a fog on all her reality.

A nurse walks quietly into the room to check on Amara. She approaches the monitor next to her. The nurse scrolls through a few options on the screen and then updates her chart with the new information. The detective rests placidly in her hospital bed. The lights in her room are low; the machines around her pump and beep in rhythm. She is sustained.

I advance down the hallway undetected and scour the way forward on my belly. I can sense her, *feel* her. I'm coming closer and closer. My anticipation reaches its zenith as I spot the nurse heading out of Amara's room. I pause to the left of the doorway along the wall. The nurse is staring down at her chart as she crosses through the door. The woman doesn't notice my presence; she continues scribbling something on her clipboard and turns right down the hall.

Completely unobstructed now, I make my entry into Amara's room. She's unaware and unperturbed as I glide against the cold tile floor. I slither toward her as my forked tongue tastes the absorbing air around us. I traverse the floor and begin wrapping myself around the legs of her hospital bed.

Round and round I go until my body reaches the right-side handrail. I press myself forward until my head caresses her torso. Then I gather the rest of my body on the hospital bed. I slink forward with caution as I collect myself into a spool atop her chest. Her breath comes strained with my weight pressed against her. My black and yellow eyes are filled with hate; they pierce holes into her unsuspecting flesh.

I continue watching Amara for a moment longer. Her docile expression provides me with some fleeting sense of peace; it offers the simple reassurance that my undertaking has all been worthwhile. As the detective labors more and more with every breath, she grows somewhat restless beneath me. Her head moves gently on its swivel as her chest rises and falls.

Amara's eyes begin to flutter as she jumps from one dream into another. When she turns her head toward me, it isn't panic that I see in her eyes. Her calm, pervasive dread is something else entirely. She opens her lips to speak, but before her words come, the room is overtaken by a plume of black, fetid smoke.

The cloud and the brimstone do not last long, but they leave a new form in their wake. I am me again, polished and refined. No longer the serpent, I stand by her bedside dutifully. There's no more blood, and I have all my fingers again. I'm wearing my black suit once more, and the rose from earlier has materialized within my grasp.

The air clears entirely. Amara stares up at me in alarm. I hold the rose with my left hand and reach the other toward her. She recoils with big, frightened eyes. She tries sitting up, but the wound causes her too much distress. My newfound power won't allow her escape. Amara freezes in the corner of her hospital bed, clutching her shoulder.

I see her fearful eyes searching for an exit plan. She starts to scream, so I place my hand on her mouth and press down. She's scanning the room and fighting against me now. I see her fingers grasping toward something on the bed panel next to her. It's a little red button with black letters above that read, "Push for Help."

I snatch Amara's hand away from it and strangle her with both hands. The rose's stem grates against her throat as she writhes beneath my pressure. As I tighten my grip, my eyes start to change. They're black marble, cold and dense. She meets my gaze with horror, and I feel her struggle diminish.

Something clicks inside of her while she weakens beneath my grasp. Her hands still clasp mine as they're wrapped around her throat, but there's no fight left. Her fingers sit placidly atop my hand as we stare into each other's eyes.

Amara's eyes begin to change as well. They shift into a solid black at first, but then the texture turns. Her black marble begins to bleed. She weeps silent streams of visceral gore; they run down her cheeks while her mouth hangs open.

She's not going anywhere. I release my hold and stand upright again. Amara stares absently into the ceiling, and it is only now that I realize something—she's dead. Her machines tell me so. There is no pulse, no sensation whatsoever. She's flatlined. And yet, something about her horror-stricken eyes convinces me that this is not so.

I study her as I adjust the wrinkles in my suit. Then I step closer to the bed, admiring her lifeless beauty. I fix the rose's petals and make them pristine once again. Leaning down, I place it upon her chest. My hand lingers there a moment before sliding to her chin.

As I caress her face, she turns slowly toward me. Her eyes have stopped bleeding, but the dark streams upon her cheeks remain. I can see that she's lucid as life works its way back inside of her. Before she can speak, I place my finger upon her lips. Her black eyes stare with intensity as I look upon her.

The room catches fire. It starts in the corners and spreads with a great flare. It travels up and down the walls and engulfs the ceiling. Amara doesn't break eye contact when the floor begins to tremble. The room is stripped to bones; its underlying frame and structure start to burn. It threatens to swallow us both, but the all-consuming chaos still cannot draw our focus.

We've surrendered to each other at last. I gaze upon my love as the room turns to blackened inferno. The ground beneath us begins to crack and shift. Drywall turns to craggy rock. All is devoured by the endless flame. Our clothes tatter and turn to ash under its scorching heat.

The descent has finally begun. She and I enter the abyss together now, a pair of wispy embers trailing to parts unknown.